IN THE DARK

DEBBI VOISEY

BLOODHOUND
— BOOKS —

The right of Debbi Voisey to be identified as the Author of the Work has been asserted by them in accordance with the Copyright, Designs and Patents Act 1988.

First published in 2025 by Bloodhound Books.

www.bloodhoundbooks.com

Print ISBN: 9781917449953

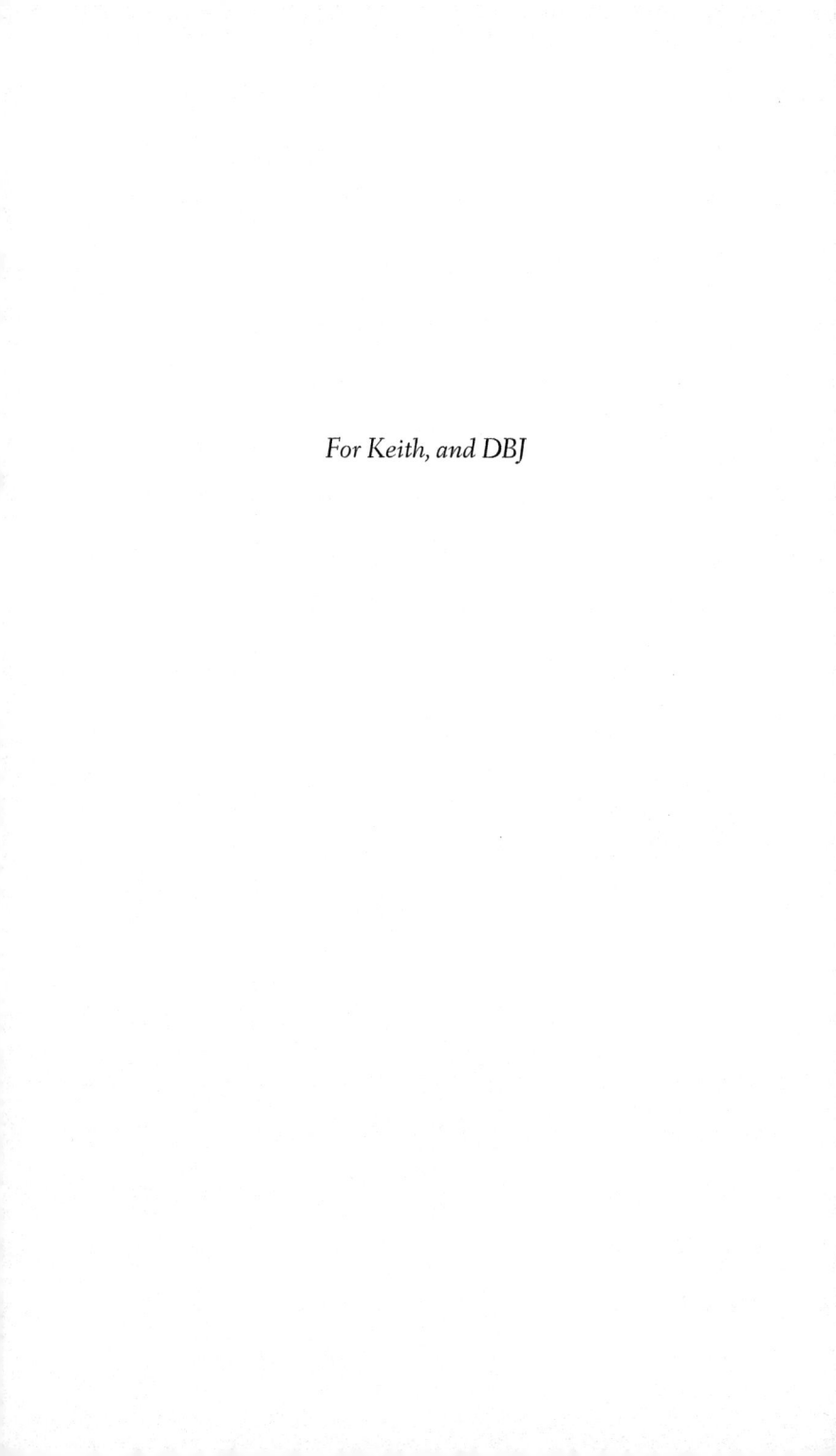

For Keith, and DBJ

PROLOGUE

She feels the fingers in her throat before her eyes have even opened, and when she does open them, she's staring into the toilet bowl and there are blobs of red foamy stuff dripping into it, connected by mucus strings to her mouth. She hears a retching she knows must be coming from her, but it sounds a million miles away. She can hear a voice coming from somewhere far away too. It sounds like her dad. Where is he? Is this him holding her? Are these his fingers?

There's a pain inside her so great it scares her. It's not just physical, not just of her body; it's profound and guttural and of her soul. It's running rampage inside her deepest parts, and she's terrified it'll rip her apart.

'Get it up, Maggie. That's it.' Not her dad but her paternal granddad, sounding so like him it tears her heart open and, as if punctuation to his words, the foamy red stuff comes in greater waves. She feels her body giving it up, ejecting it; whatever is inside her. It's like lava from an angry volcano. It's red, and it's heavy, and it's full of lumps.

And then she remembers: diazepam and red wine. The former she can't remember how many; the latter she knows two bottles. She vaguely remembers sinking onto these cold bathroom tiles and wanting it all to go away; the pain of missing her dad as she has every night for the last seventeen years. The pain of messing everything up so badly with Paul, today of all days, when they were supposed to be so happy. And the pain of losing Charlie. That will never go away. She remembers wanting it all to stop, and believing the pills and the wine would make it.

But she's being dragged back by this man she now loves best in the world. She hates that he won the title by default. He doesn't deserve her thinking that way.

'I needed him then, and I need him now.' She thinks she's saying this out loud as her granddad lays her on the bed and covers her with the duvet. He sits beside her, and the kind face that has her father's eyes is streaked with lines of worry. She's so ashamed she's put this man, who's eighty-seven, through this. Even as the room lurches and swirls and her stomach flips, she still has the presence to feel ashamed.

'I'm so sorry, Maggie. I let you down,' he says.

But she fears she's done the same to him.

1

_____

NOW – TWELVE YEARS LATER

Every morning around 7am when Maggie Milburn wakes, the bear is hunched at the end of her bed, its teeth dripping albumen-like goop onto the duvet that is always scrunched up due to her thrashing about. Nightmares have become an almost-nightly event, but Maggie can never be sure if the bear is part of them, or an actual breathing thing. It *feels* real, and often in the silent small hours of morning, she can hear it panting; its huge lungs sucking the air and the sanity out of her room.

Her nightmares are sometimes disguised as harmless dreams of *that* place, beautiful and scenic, nestled in the foothills of Scafell Pike. Tents scattered through the camp, excited girls and boys, wind howling and blowing everything away except their spirits. Beans for breakfast then onward; adventure round the corner. Only, it wasn't just adventure waiting. It was something more. Something dangerous.

When she'd got back home and told her mum about the bear, she'd laughed and said there were no bears in the Lake District; told her not to be silly. So, for a while she doubted herself and wondered if that half-remembered breath on her neck – that hairy weight that had pushed her face down into the sleeping bag so hard she could taste nylon – was real. But what came after proved it.

She opens a window to let more air in, and to let out the fetid bear-stench.

She tried to tell her therapist about the bear once. It hadn't gone as she'd hoped:

'A bear, you say?'

'Yes, a bear.'

'Brown or grizzly? Or polar?'

'Does it matter? It's a bear. In my bedroom every night. The breed is irrelevant.'

'Nothing is irrelevant, Maggie.' Notes scratched onto the pad.

The fucking pad. Maggie had grown to loathe it.

The therapist had wanted to explore the bear, but all Maggie had wanted was for him to say the bear wasn't real. That the reason for it was... and then something that made sense.

But all her therapist wanted to do was dig into it.

Maggie didn't.

'Maybe it's a spectacled bear.' More scribbling. A smug, self-congratulatory grunt.

Fuck the fucking bear. Maggie didn't care if it wore glasses or not.

She steps over the bear's leg to get to the wardrobe. Her only goals for this morning are to get dressed and work on the project for Monday. Also, if she does manage to put clothes on and can keep them clean, she'll visit her grandfather and see if her grandmother needs help with him. The time is getting near, she has come to realise with a heavy heart.

This morning, yellow sun rays are pouring in through the slats of the blinds. She can see every individual hair in the bear's pelt. It reminds her of that thing she wants to forget. Seeing the hairs, imagining the texture, takes her back to that place she doesn't want to revisit, so she digs her heels in mentally and tries not to think.

Thinking is bad. Thinking always stops her functioning. That won't do.

She's holding her breath; will do so until the bear leaves. It always leaves.

But it always comes back.

2

———————

NOW

The kitchen is drenched in sunshine and as she stands at the sink filling the kettle, she closes her eyes and allows the warmth of it to wash over her face.

When she was younger, the sun always signified long school holidays because she'd go out in it soon after breakfast and not come back until it was westward bound. No one worried back then. No one's mum rang the police, or stood on the front step wringing their hands and wailing that their child was lost. Sometimes her mum hardly noticed she was gone until she returned, smeared in dirt and grime from head to foot, breathless with the ravages of adventure and the long hours of the day.

She supposes her mum had her own worries to see to back then. The bills, her two jobs to *pay* those bills. Making ends – and sanity – meet.

Today, the sun is making grid patterns from the window panels on her kitchen worktop. She takes a nectarine from the fridge and stands it in the rays between the lines, so the chill of the fridge will leave before she eats it at lunchtime. She makes coffee, and thinks of her dad, who always liked three cups before he allowed any food to pass his lips.

A year before he'd succumbed to the cancer, he'd taken six-year-old Maggie to Blackpool. Just the two of them because her mum was busy, and the first stop they'd made was to a café just off the promenade. The sun had been blazing through the plate glass window and Maggie had had to squint at her dad in the chair opposite her, his back to it.

It's all suddenly so clear she has to hold on to the edge of the sink. Thirty years ago, and it feels like yesterday. She wonders when it will stop, this drifting back to the past.

3

THEN

'Let's see how many donuts we can eat today, Mags,' her dad says, and her heart soars like it's attached to a kite and her whole being wants to burst into a thousand rainbow-coloured stars. These are the kinds of challenges they do when her dad is in a playful mood. Sausages at breakfast, burgers at tea; they shovel them in and her mum pretends to be mad but keeps them coming regardless.

So they sit, drenched in sunshine, with sugar all over their mouths, tears of mirth turning it to syrup, and she wants to stay like this forever.

Then her dad wipes the tears and sugar granules off his face with a napkin and says: 'I have something I need to tell you, and you have to be a big brave girl.'

So she is brave. On the surface. She doesn't want her dad to feel bad, or as if he's scared her. She brushes the sugar off her face and sits up really straight, like her mother always insists she do at the dinner table. She faces him head on and her gaze doesn't waver, not even when the door opens and a woman comes in carrying the cutest pug. Maggie has always wanted a pug. She can see him wriggling out of the corner of her eye, but she keeps her focus on her dad.

'Okay, Daddy. Don't be scared. Tell me.'

'I'm not well, my darling. I have cancer. Do you know what that is?'

Maggie isn't sure exactly, but she knows it's bad because one of the girls in class had a grandfather who'd had it and he died not long ago. A cold fear creeps over her, like she feels when she has to go to the toilet at night, which is downstairs. She doesn't like the shadows in there, or how cold it is, or those spiders with the tiny dot bodies and legs thin as hairs.

She shakes her head.

'Listen, darling,' her dad says gently, reaching out and grabbing her hand. 'It means I have something... a condition... that will make me sick for a while. And I'll need to go to the hospital a few times and have some medicine. It might make me look different for a bit.'

'Different? How?'

'Sometimes it makes people lose their hair. But I've started to go bald already so you might not notice, eh?' He laughs, but Maggie doesn't.

He tells her not to worry too much, because today he's feeling right as rain, and they're going to finish their donuts and go and lie on the sand and shovel as many shrimps out of a cone and into their gobs as they can.

So they do. They lie down and make sand angels and Maggie doesn't even worry that her hair is full of grains or that she can see little crabs scuttling a few feet away, and they argue about who gets to wear the Kiss Me Quick hat. One of the rules of the game – as her dad now explains to her – is whoever is wearing it has to approach anyone wearing red and ask for a kiss. Neither of them actually has the nerve to do it, but every time someone wearing red walks by her dad nudges her and walks behind the person, matching his footsteps to theirs and puckering his lips like he's going to kiss them. They both laugh so hard because the person in front could turn around at any moment, and her dad's laugh is the most wonderful sound in the world.

They travel in silence most of the way down the motorway, listening to Paul Simon on the car stereo. Her dad is tapping on the steering wheel in time to the song.

It's an almost perfect day in every way, apart from when her dad told her he's sick and she thought about her friend's grandfather dying. And the worry that's started to take hold now the fun is over.

'You're going to get better, aren't you, Daddy?' She asks this for the first time. He doesn't take his eyes off the road.

'Of course, Maggie darling,' he says, and she wants to believe him. She does.

But in less than a year he's going to be proved a liar.

4

NOW

She needs to get the project paperwork completed, so she decides that after breakfast and the Sunday papers she'll get to it. Her therapist says she needs to keep busy. He says having something to focus on aids healing. Something that's healthy though, not destructive.

She told him about her big project at her last session, and he said that sounded just the ticket and made notes in his pad. Maggie asked him if alcohol could be considered something healthy to focus on too, and laughed when she said it to let him know she was joking. But she was only half joking, and she really wanted him to say 'yes, that's something really healthy, keep it up'.

But of course, he didn't say that. He just looked at her over his glasses, as if she was a schoolkid who'd just fired an ink pellet. The school image brought her too close, far too close, to the thing she wants to forget, so she backed away and told him she was joking, and he just went back to making his notes.

The papers say there's been issues with social media sites, and some people are reporting data losses. Apparently, it's been an intermittent problem and is being looked into. Users are assured the problems will be addressed and normal service resumed as soon as possible, and in the meantime, let's see what the Kardashians are up to this week.

When enough time has passed for it to be considered 'decent', she opens a bottle of Malbec. She can never look at bridal stuff, flowers, and centrepieces without a glass of the good stuff in front of her. At one time, she thought that would be her, wearing the gown and marrying her love, but that's been fucked up. *She's* fucked it up, is the truth.

Because she can't shake off that fucking bear.

So now she tortures herself arranging other people's weddings, but it's strangely comforting to see people succeed at the one thing she thinks will be denied her. That she's denying herself.

She's *almost* bagged a client who wants to arrange weddings for five of his nieces. This is huge – another swig of Malbec is in order – and something that makes her heart race. She's made a 'mood board' of designs for all five weddings, secured appointments at the best wedding venues in the county via their online booking platforms, and just needs to finalise florist, caterer and chauffeur contracts, or at least the promise of them.

She polishes off another glass while rehearsing for her presentation tomorrow. She considers lunch, but instead decides on snacks and more wine. It's not a good idea. It never is. One glass always leads to two, then three, then – poof! – the day is gone, and all that stands between her and the next day is a headache and that fucking bear.

So she calls for a taxi, needing her gramps and not knowing why. She decides to use the landline since her Uber app will probably not be working and she just wants to get there as quickly as possible. The despatcher – a grumpy sounding Welsh woman – tells her it could be forty minutes because everyone is out and it's the weekend of Eid, so most of the drivers are off.

She grabs another glass of wine and sits on the sofa, going through her figures again.

Her mobile rings, startling her, and she snatches it up. The caller ID screen is inexplicably wavy, like it's going to go kaput any moment, but she sees *PAUL* and she hesitates just for a beat before answering.

'I'm just running out the door,' she says in greeting and hears his snort of a laugh, the one that's just a breath of air down his nose. The one he always does when he's ready to take no shit.

'Charming, Mags. At least give me two minutes before blowing me off.'

'Sorry, I'm going to see my granddad. It's been a long day.'

She doesn't need this. Hearing from Paul is always painful, even though it's been over twelve years since they dated and they've seen each other quite a few times since, just as friends, to prove – if only to themselves – all is okay. Well, they dated then got engaged, then planned the wedding, then did the stag and hen, then woke up on their wedding day, then...

'Mags, did you hear what I said?' Paul stops her thoughts in their tracks. 'Do you fancy a drink sometime in the week? Thursday or Friday is good for me. I'll bring the boys so you can meet them at last. It's Aaron's birthday and I have them both the whole week. Thought it might be nice. Catch up? I haven't seen you for months.'

'The boys?' Her voice sounds strangled to her own ears. She doesn't know if she can bear to see them but knows she must. She can't avoid them forever if she wants to remain friends with Paul. It's stupid anyway, what happened is not Paul's or his sons' fault.

'It'll be okay, I promise,' he says, as if he's read her mind. 'And if it's not, if I get an inkling you're not, we'll leave. Okay?'

'Okay...' She's hesitant but agrees. 'It'll have to be Thursday, though, I have a date on Friday.' She can practically hear his eyebrow raising.

Her phone starts to make strangled noises and her landline rings once; the taxi is outside, earlier than they said.

'I have to go, Paul. I'll call you early next week.'

'Okay, Mags. Say hi to Harold for me. I miss that guy. I hope he's—'

The mobile cuts out. Maggie's relieved because she can't bear to hear what he was going to say. Paul doesn't know how ill he's become.

She misses her granddad too. So much. And he's not even dead yet.

5

NOW

Aaron Griffiths has hidden his phone in his sock drawer. He feels it'll be safe in there; that *he* will be safe from *it*. The fabric of all his rolled-up socks will muffle everything and keep it quiet. His phone hasn't been quiet for months. He can't bear it anymore.

His mum doesn't want him to have a phone, says he's too young and phones are nothing but trouble. He heard her arguing with his dad about it the last time he'd dropped him off after taking him to football, and at the time he'd been so happy because his dad had won the argument and his mum had given in.

To Aaron, having a phone is a magical thing. All the other kids in his class have them. Some even have the latest models because their parents have great jobs. One of the lads in his class has a dad who's a footballer. Not City or United, just County, but they sometimes show their matches on the telly, so he always gets the latest stuff. All the boys huddled around him when he got his and he'd proudly shown it off. An Android, he'd told them, which made it sound like one of those robots from the sci-fi films Aaron loves to watch. The camera on it is amazing, so they always take lots of great photos of things like arm wrestling matches and scuffles of all different kinds.

When Aaron's dad took him into town to buy one of his own it was the most exciting day of his life. They'd gone into the Arndale, stood in a queue a mile long in Carphone Warehouse, and left with a brilliant gun-metal grey Samsung S9, which he knows is even better than the footballer's son's. Then after that, his dad had taken him to Costa for a hot chocolate with a flake and it had been all he could do not to get the phone out in the café. The bag felt red hot against his leg, he was so eager to play with it.

When they'd got home, his dad had had to stay longer to help him set it up, so that led to him having tea with them, and his mum and dad even got along a little better than usual. A perfect day.

The phone is all very exciting. Until the messages start coming in on the Fantastic Year Five! WhatsApp group someone at school has set up so people can talk about weekend football and proposed trips into town. They are okay at first, the messages. Just a bit of banter. Kids he knows from his class, and some from other classes in his year. Most of the boys are cool; he wishes he was like many of them. But some of them – even the ones he worships – have become nasty and cruel.

@Griffiths_Aaron: What's it like with no dad?

@Griffiths_Aaron: Your mum looking 4 a new boyfriend?

@Griffiths_Aaron: Spazzy orphan kid.

@Griffiths_Aaron: You're fucking dead, nancy boy

None of the texts are even right. Aaron knows this because orphaned means both parents being dead, but his are both still alive just not living together. He still has a dad, and his mum isn't looking for a new boyfriend – as far as he knows. He knows the people who sent those messages are stupid, and they pass it off as 'bants' when he sees them in school. He tries to laugh when they're there; fearful of what will happen if he doesn't. But he spends most of his breaks locked in a toilet cubicle, trembling and not eating his lunch, which he knows will make him sick if he tries because his stomach is in knots.

And it gets worse, and it starts to hurt, because they now say such horrible things about his mum and threaten him and his little brother.

And suddenly, life is dark and scary.

6

NOW

Frances Jones watches the second hand tick, tick, tick its way round the clock. She's never noticed before, but the face has a pearly sheen to it, and it looks like the inside of the shells she used to collect on Blackpool sands with her mum and dad when she was a nipper.

When the second hand has done the circuit 120 times, her husband, Steve, will be back from the pub. She prepares his dinner. He keeps telling her to call it lunch; that calling it dinner makes her sound like the council estate scum she is, but she doesn't want to lose herself. Doesn't want him to strip away every part of her. So, she puts his dinner of chicken and roast potatoes into the oven. She knows how long, and how many circuits of the clock are left, and when she finishes her chores to make him pleased – or not make him *displeased* – she sits back on the sofa and won't move until that 120th trip around the seashell face.

Looking at the sheen of the clock, as iridescent as the shells she used to put against her ear at the seaside, memories come flooding.

'Frances, mind you don't burn your feet. Put your shoes on.'

Memories so vivid and so real she can hear her mother's voice, which has the timbre of a soprano.

She wishes she had sand to burn her feet now. She wishes she was back in the time that had been so uncomplicated. She wishes her mum was here, holding her hand and telling her everything was going to be all right, that all the despair she's feeling will go away. But her mum is in London and Frances would never tell her anyway. She's never told another living soul.

She picks up her phone and taps on the betting app; has to do it five times before it opens. It's shimmering like a ghost and the Ace of Spades and Queen of Hearts dance in front of her eyes as if underwater. She realises it's probably her tears doing that, and she has no idea when she started crying. She's feeling a loss so deep and is so far down in a pit she doesn't think she can ever crawl out of it.

When he walks through the door, he's staggering a little. His jacket is off and his sleeves rolled up, and a half-depleted six pack of Carling is dangling from his right index finger. Through the Venetian blinds, slats of Sunday afternoon sunlight are streaking across his face and he looks like a warrior. A warrior come for his woman. There's a smile on his face.

That smile is always the most terrifying thing. She's come to fear it more than anything.

He throws his jacket and the cans onto his armchair, then lunges towards the sofa. His lips are wet and there's a yellowy-brown stain down the front of his shirt – probably a curry, from that place that does Sunday lunch curries. So he won't be wanting his dinner then. He never texts to let her know. More often than not, he eats before coming home and doesn't want his dinner, but if she didn't have it ready for him, she'd be in trouble. She found that out once. The now-legendary 'day of the glass vase'.

She still has a scar from it on her jawline.

He'll sleep first, before launching the inevitable onslaught. A snooze that will last a few hours. Maybe even, if she's lucky, until the morning.

Enough time to finish a whole bottle of gin and disappear into oblivion.

A strangled warble from her phone interrupts her an hour later, mid-bottle. She doesn't recognise the sound because it is so different and odd, but it's a text message, barely visible, slowly fading out. She just about makes out it's from Susan, someone she has a laugh with at the gym, in her spinning class.

> Fancy a bottle at Spoons? Got a kid and hubby free night. 6pm? Know it's early but I'm in the mood. All my real friends said no! LOL

Frances looks at the seashell clock. It's 4pm. Her husband is out cold, but she doesn't know for how long. Should she risk it?

> Bitch. LOL. How about now? This fake friend needs a fucking drink STAT!

She takes care and time with her make-up, can't afford any questions. She applies her foundation extra thick.

7

NOW

The room always smells of Algipan and Gramps's herbal tablets; those golden oblong sugar-encrusted lozenges that taste like aniseed and school holidays. Whenever she smells them on the breath of passing strangers, she wants to follow them and tell them about her grandfather and how he liberated not only hundreds of Jews, but also her. At ninety-nine, he's fourteen years older than her gran. Everyone always thought he'd get his telegram from the Queen, but this isn't going to happen. They all know this now.

He went to war long before he met his wife, refusing to 'step out', as he called it, with anyone until his duty was done. He met Maggie's gran when he was thirty-three and she was nineteen, seven years after he'd returned from northern Germany. It had taken that long for him to sufficiently start to heal and even contemplate a relationship.

He told Maggie once, and only once, that seeing what the Nazis had done to humans was the most harrowing thing anyone could witness. He'd killed men during his service and seen limbs blown off his friends. But seeing a person starved to the point where their bones and internal organs were evident under paper-thin skin was more terrible than anything he'd seen before or has seen since.

His hands have fired rifles that took people's lives, but they've also stroked Maggie's hair when she's lain foetus-like on her bathroom floor. Arms that once carried dead comrades have rocked her into a sleep that pushes away the visions the daylight can't mask.

She knows she wouldn't be alive without him. Doesn't know how she'll survive after him.

Though he never talks about his experiences, she sees them etched on his face. His brow is always furrowed, like he's looking into the distance and seeing horrors, and she knows – in her breaking heart – that the image he sees now as he lies in his bed, is going to be one of the final ones.

Maggie's gran dips a sage-green flannel in the bowl of water she had Maggie fetch from the kitchen, wrings it, gently lays it on her husband's forehead. A teardrop of water runs onto the pillow. It's impossible to tell if it's from the flannel or his eye.

'Sage green is your colour,' her gran says to him, although he probably isn't listening. Waking nightmares have stolen his senses these last few days, as if finally, after all these years, he can't take any more. He doesn't hear or see, and only rarely responds to anything outside the confines of his mind. But still Maggie's gran bathes his face and talks to him about the life they had together. Because sometimes, when they're blessed, he comes back briefly.

She mops the brow of the man she's spent sixty-six years with, had four children, ten grandchildren and twenty-one great-grandchildren with. The man who went to war and fought as bravely and humanely as he could, because he needed to help make a world his family would feel safe in, and that he could feel proud to say he had a hand in forming.

'I loved him in his army fatigues,' she says to Maggie.

'Although, he always told me it wasn't sage green, but army green. But whatever colour it was, he was so handsome. I have pictures, although of course the green is grey in those old photos. Like most things now. The colour is being sucked from everything, now he's leaving.'

'I've seen them, Gran.' Maggie's voice is flat and monotone. 'I have one as my Facebook cover photo.'

'Oh, show me,' her gran says. Maggie reaches for her bag and brings out her phone.

She thinks it's funny how times have changed, and how technology has seeped into every aspect of life. A thousand photos in your hand, on a small contraption you carry in your bag or your pocket. And no one ever looks at them. All those loved ones and memories of days you want to treasure, and you take it for granted. Because, you think, they'll always be there.

You can look at them tomorrow.

Her granddad is in here, embedded in metal and glass and a SIM card. If these phones had been around in his day, maybe the horrors of the war wouldn't have occurred because people would've known what was happening and when, and rapidly held people to account. She wants to think that, but isn't sure if it's true. Technology might not have changed anything really, because people will always be people. There've been wars since. There'll be wars again.

She places her fingertip on the screen and it bursts into brightness. There's nothing on it except a green colour that's the same hue as the flannel on her gramps's forehead; the same colour as his army fatigues. She swipes a finger over it. Nothing happens. She turns the screen on and off by the button on the side.

No icons. No Facebook, no Twitter, no Safari.

'That's funny, Gran. I think my phone's on the blink.'

'Oh, I wanted to see the photo of him in his uniform.'

Maggie wants to see it too. She scrolls down from it every time she opens Facebook, which is about a million times a day, and can't remember the last time she'd actually *seen* it. That youthful face, the expectation and hope that had gradually been stripped from him. She can't help the feeling washing over her that time is slipping through her fingers like sand and soon, too soon, her gramps will be scattered like ashes amongst the grains.

'We can look at it tomorrow, Gran,' she says. She doesn't know that won't be possible.

8

NOW

There have only been three times in Aaron's short life he's ever been truly afraid.

The first time was when he was six and he'd got lost in the woods on a camping holiday with his mum, dad and brother. They'd been playing hide-and-seek and he'd been showing off, thinking he could find his way around, wandering off farther than he should. His mum and dad had ended up frantic and he remembers the fierceness of his mum's hug when they eventually found him, and the wetness of her tears running down his neck. Until he figured out his way back, his imagination had played terrible tricks on him, and he believed he'd never see his family again. That he'd die in the tangle of trees on the springy ground beneath his feet. He'd imagined a search party that would find his body crawling with ants and his bones sticking out through lack of food. He'd truly believed he was a goner.

The second time he was afraid wasn't so long ago, when his mum and dad had split up. They'd been arguing a lot for a while, and life at home had been no fun for anyone. He and George would be sent upstairs to their room while the battle went on downstairs, and they'd almost grown accustomed to it. They'd play games like I Spy or Battleships on paper, or tell each other spooky stories. Anything to pass the time.

This one day, they were playing pirates on the bed – Aaron was of course making George walk the plank – when the arguing downstairs stopped; became a silence that stretched out too long. Aaron had crept to the top of the stairs and had seen a suitcase sitting by the front door. Beside it, his dad's legs, and he heard the keys and change in his dad's pocket as he put on his coat.

Aaron had run downstairs to find his mum with tears running down her cheeks; his dad red-faced.

'Where are you going?' Aaron had wailed, and his dad had told him he was going away but it didn't mean he didn't love him, and he must be a good boy for his mum and make sure George went to bed on time every night.

And Aaron had asked how many nights, and his dad had told him he didn't know.

He'd clung on to his dad's leg and begged him not to go, not to go, not to go, over and over, until his mum had to help prise his fingers away, and his dad had left without a backward glance.

Aaron's greatest fear was being the oldest boy in the house, and he didn't know what to do without his dad, the man who looked after everything and made everyone feel safe. Who'd lock the doors? Who'd remove the spiders for his screaming mum? Who'd change the plugs?

They've all adjusted as a family; they're *still* a family, but a different one. His dad lives in a house not too far away and they see him often. His mum seems happier, calmer, less tearful. It's certainly quieter in their house, with no fighting and shouting. And the best thing: as if in compensation, Aaron and his brother get spoiled a lot more by both parents. So, life isn't too bad.

Until the messages started coming, bringing with them the third time Aaron has felt real fear.

People at school have been talking about the actress Stephanie Wilson a lot; the one who was in a soap and was getting slaughtered on social media. All his mates think it's hilarious, but he'd found his mum crying about it one night. He'd asked her why she was upset, and she'd told him people can be so cruel and judgemental, and until they've walked in someone's shoes, they shouldn't comment on someone's life choices. Aaron doesn't really understand what his mum was on about. All he knows is everyone is calling the actress a skank. He doesn't know what that means, but he does know a thing or two about being singled out, pestered, relentlessly messaged and bullied.

When the outages come – when TikTok and Snapchat stop working and the WhatsApp group stops bouncing every thirty seconds – the silence is the most beautiful sound he's ever heard in his short life. He can breathe again. He can get out of bed in the morning and look forward to the day, because without the anonymity of technology and the ability to hide behind their keypads, no one at school is owning up to anything and everyone is keeping their head down. It's like it never happened.

9

NOW

At home Maggie phones Franny at 8pm, while crunching sour cream and onion Pringles. Frances (Franny) Jones has been her joined-at-the-hip best friend since school. It made perfect sense for them to become business partners because they know each other so well. They often don't need words to communicate, which comes in really handy at meetings with clients. What looks like the mere lifting of an eyebrow to the uninitiated can mean anything from *Who the fuck is this joker?* to *Put the bubbly on ice, we have this in the bag!* depending on how high it's raised or how arched it is. It's a language you can't teach anyone else, you just have to have lived it for years.

'How's your grandfather?' Franny asks.

Bless her, Maggie thinks. *She never forgets.* 'Not good, I'm afraid. It won't be long now.'

'I'm so sorry, Mags. Hang on, let me get another drink and we can talk.'

Franny sounds sad. It's also noisy where she is. She's obviously not at home.

'Are you out? Not like you on a school night.'

'Susan texted me. You know, Megathighs from spin class.

Her kids are at their grandparents with their dad, so she wanted to make a bid for freedom.'

'Oh well, I won't keep you.'

'But, Mags, your granddad...'

'It's fine. It'll keep. I'll be seeing you tomorrow anyway.'

'Will you be okay tonight?'

'Oh sure, you know me. Bottle of wine will see me right.'

Maggie doesn't want to tell her the bear is here today. Whenever she mentions it, Franny worries. She doesn't like her being alone in the house with her mind troubled like that. She never disputes the bear is real, at least for Maggie. But her concern is always palpable.

But Maggie doesn't have to worry about mentioning the bear anyway, because after a couple of minutes her phone cuts off and she's left looking at that empty sage-green screen again.

As she brushes her teeth while getting ready for bed, Maggie watches the water going down the plughole in swirls. It's a myth that it goes clockwise here and anti-clockwise in Australia. Her dad had believed it and told her it does, but apart from that, he knows everything. *Knew* everything, she has to correct her thoughts at once. He knew about all kinds of weird natural phenomena, like wave propagation, tidal flow, lunar rainbows, blood moons, midnight sun and polar night.

She can't remember the word for the effect that made people believe about the sink thing. Her dad would know – *would have known*, damn it. It's still hard, even after twenty-nine years without him, to think of him in the past tense because inside her, he's always present.

When he'd been at the funeral home, her mum had told her not to go to the viewing. Said he didn't look the way she'd have remembered him. But she went and was glad because he'd looked peaceful and like there was some kind of light shining into the coffin onto his face. He'd looked like a man who'd wrung all the great things out of life despite his young age and was satisfied there was nothing left.

As she dries her hands she remembers: *Coriolis force*.

She turns the tap on again and watches the water swirl away. Tonight, she'll check for moonbows and falling stars, and hopes if they're there, her dad will see them too.

10

NOW

The bear's asleep when she goes to bed. There's not a peep from him. He's always quiet and well-behaved whenever she comes back from visiting her granddad, almost as if he knows he's no match for the love Maggie gets from him.

Maggie recalls the day the bear started visiting her at home. It was on her sixteenth birthday. It was hiding behind the armchair her mum had put her present on. Only a cub then, it had been making sounds like kitten purrs and lying dormant, almost in supplication. It looked cute, but Maggie didn't fail to notice it had long needle-like claws and tiny but sharp fangs.

She'd moved her present – she can't remember what it was, but maybe a handbag she'd had her eye on – and the chair wobbled, eliciting grunts from the bear. She'd shot a look at her mum as if to ask, *what the heck is a bear doing there?* but her mum was acting like nothing was out of the ordinary.

Being sixteen was a stressful time. She had felt under pressure having to compete with all the other sixteen-year-olds in her class, and watching the future come running towards her full pelt. Career guidance counsellors had been telling her she was destined for a future in factory work, or office work if she was lucky. Gender stereotyping had been the norm, and no one was allowed to think outside the box. And besides, they took great pleasure in telling her she should count herself lucky she hadn't been thrown out of school after what happened four years previously. A terrible business it was, and she had to hope and pray to God she'd be allowed to put it behind her and find a job like a good girl.

In retrospect, her life back then was a perfect storm into which the bear lumbered and made his den. He'd just snuggled down like cubs do, as if for winter, and for a long time she'd not had much trouble from him. But he'd grown, because nothing can lie dormant forever. Eventually you have to face it.

And now he's here most nights and most mornings. It's something she's developing coping mechanisms for with the help of her therapist. It's not easy, but she'll get there. And even though Franny worries for her, she knows she can be relied on if things get too much and she needs to talk.

Paul has always known; she introduced him to the bear a long time ago. He's been a rock in her life, and has stuck around despite her attempts to push him away. Not that she ever pushed him deliberately, it just turned out that way. When she met him, she'd thought he'd be the answer to everything. To not having a man in her life who exerted a positive influence, like her dad always did.

And he was almost the answer. The first few months he had been the tonic her body and mind had been craving. He helped her forget men could be so loved and yet so absent, or so hated and yet present.

Because he'd been the complete and positive mix of those two things: he was loved, and he was here.

11

THEN

Maggie's body is a prisoner released. Here, in the place she feels safe because everyone is a freak like her with more baggage than Manchester Airport, she can be herself. No one cares. No one is looking.

Except maybe for the one guy, standing at the bar.

The music from the jukebox is doing things to her limbs. It's making them fluid and soft, and for the first time in ages she's not rigid and closed up. Franny has persuaded her to dance, here at their regular haunt, The Cage, and they're both drunk enough that it's fun, but not too drunk they'll fall over or crash into tables.

The guy is still watching. He's handsome in a quirky way. Not drop-dead gorgeous, but the kind of good-looking a girl can feel safe with. He has straight, floppy hair that keeps falling into his face, and every time he pushes it back, Maggie is struck by his intense eyes. They're not scary though, if she can still be a judge of that kind of thing after three large glasses of red.

Franny is watching him closely, and moves herself nearer to Maggie as they dance, turning her body into a shield between her and the guy. She's very protective over Maggie, for many reasons. She's witnessed all the traumas down the years. She's not prepared to allow anyone to add more to the list.

But Maggie has other ideas, and whispers into Franny's ear: 'Let him pass, comrade. I'll be okay.'

As she approaches the bar, on which he's leaning with his left elbow, she says, 'You can buy me a drink if you like.' He raises one eyebrow as if amused. Without a word to Maggie, he asks the barman for a large glass of red.

He's wearing a black leather jacket and pale blue denims with worn patches at the thighs. He produces money from a battered leather wallet, which inexplicably makes Maggie smile. Most of the men she's dated lately carry their loose change around in their pockets, along with snotty tissues and packets of gum. She likes this considered approach to money organisation. It's a little old-fashioned to her, but she likes it.

She feels a flush come to her cheeks as he hands her the wine, and their fingers brush together ever so briefly.

'Are you going to speak, or are you the strong, silent type?' Maggie asks, before taking a sip of wine. The alcohol joins the rest she's had tonight, and it slowly oozes through her bloodstream. She can almost feel it flowing through her veins.

'I like to speak only when I've something useful to offer, or something interesting to talk about,' he says, which strikes Maggie as odd, but also amusing, and she finds him very attractive, so she lets it pass.

'Oh, and does this situation pass your standards test?' she asks.

'It does, but I'm still not sure I have anything useful or interesting to say.'

'I'll be the judge of that,' Maggie says. 'I'm Maggie Milburn, and that person over the other side of the room who looks as if she's sizing you up for a body bag, is my very good friend and bodyguard, Frances Jones. She's trained in mortal combat, so she'll fight you to the death if need be. She's deadly, and she's here to keep me from harm. I just wanted to tell you that from the off, because she's never going away.'

'Fair enough. I'm happy you've such a dedicated assassin at your service.' He holds out his hand. 'I'm Paul... Griffiths... I don't have a bodyguard because generally when I see trouble coming at me, I run as fast as I can in the opposite direction. I love that you have one though. Is she available for hire?'

'She could be. Do you have the funds? I think her price is a double vodka and tonic. Maybe a series of them.'

She calls Franny over and she accepts the vodka, all the time eyeing Paul warily. But as the night progresses, she sees that Franny begins to feel he's no threat, although of course, she knows you can never be sure, not so quickly.

Maggie's pulse quickens whenever his body comes near to hers, and she hasn't felt that for a long time. She notices he's drinking Coke and asks him if he has whisky in it. He tells her he doesn't drink because he saw what kind of person his dad became whenever he'd had a few.

'He was ugly,' he says, and Maggie hears a slight tremor. 'When he drank, all bets were off.' It seems to be all he wants to say on the matter, and he sticks to the Coke.

Later, when Maggie goes to the loo, Franny squares up to Paul.

'I'm not a bitch,' she says, not giving him time to respond apart from a raised eyebrow before hurrying on. 'I promise you I'm not. But I'm prepared to become your worst nightmare if you do one thing to hurt Maggie. I'm serious. I'm talking severe physical harm.'

Paul slowly puts his glass down on the bar and pushes back the hair that has flopped into his face for the millionth time tonight. He doesn't say anything for a moment; takes in a deep breath. He tries to gauge how serious Franny is. He sees in her eyes that she's deadly so.

'I'd think badly of you if you didn't,' he said.

Paul drives Maggie home at the end of an evening of non-stop chatting and occasional dancing. It's almost impossible to get Franny to relax about the lift, but she eventually does, and allows Maggie to go with Paul while she catches a tram back by herself.

He kisses her chastely on the cheek before saying goodnight. Maggie wants him to kiss her on the mouth, and the disappointment accompanies her to bed, even as the appreciation of it warms something deep inside her.

12

NOW

The button on the kettle clicks and so does something in Franny's head. A proper click, like someone switching on a light. Something comes into view. This something is vague and blurry. She shakes the image away. All she wants is caffeine and a nice sit on the sofa to ease away the morning after the night before feeling. She's relieved Steve left early for work.

She pours water into her mug and takes a sip. It scalds her lip, and there's that light switch again. This time it shows an angry face, close to hers. It shows eyes, dark with rage, filling her own field of vision.

What the fuck? The face she's seeing is really familiar, but something is stopping her seeing it clearly, and it remains behind some hazy veil. The flashes of it are causing a strange sensation on her skin. It feels like a thousand tiny ants are crawling over it. Her stomach lurches.

She knows she had one and a half bottles of wine last night – maybe more, because she shared three bottles with Susan, and Susan drinks like a member of the temperance society; always says she doesn't need booze to be a loony. So maybe more like two bottles. And a bit. Plus, she vaguely remembers, the half-bottle of gin she drank before going out.

She knows Susan saw her into the Uber, because she'd laughed at the way she climbed in head first, crawling along the seat. She knows she got home because she's here.

But she also thinks she knows that obscured face. And she thinks it belongs to Steve.

Her first instinct is to phone Maggie, so she reaches for her phone, but when she taps on the phone icon, everything is blank. Text messages, same. She clicks on the Contacts folder and that is empty too. She's been hearing for the last twenty-four hours about a virus attacking phones and computers and wiping hard drives. Or was it a pulse? On the news they said something about it maybe being a pulse from space. It all sounds mad to Franny, and a little scary. Probably something to do with politics or war – things like that usually are. But no one is really saying anything or clarifying it.

She's relieved to find her Jackpot Jingle App is still there, and when she clicks on it, it springs to life. Just one go before leaving.

The sounds are intoxicating. Whistles and bells, whizzing, fizzing, ding ding dings. They're better than anything, those casino sounds, calling to a part of her brain that cannot resist the pull or the promises, however empty they are.

They remind Franny of the time she took her parents to Las Vegas for their first trip abroad. They'd been in awe the moment the plane landed on American soil and hadn't stopped marvelling at the size of everything – from cars, to burgers, to towering buildings – until they got back on the plane to come home.

The casino had almost finished them off. So huge it took ten minutes to walk through, if you could actually find your way. No exit signs, no directions, just comfy chairs next to gaming tables, and atomic smiles from wait staff bringing endless drinks and snacks.

To keep you rooted. To keep you spending.

The sounds of the machines had seduced her then, and she's still seduced now, by the sound effects from her app. She has to fetch her own drinks from the kitchen, but she's still rooted. Still spending. She knows, in some subconscious part of herself, that she's using gambling as a crutch, but she pushes the rationale away, because without the crutch, how else would she stand up?

The noises from her phone seem to be connected to her pulse rate. When they come fast and furious, her heart pumps quicker, taking blood and coffee to every pore. She feels the prickle of excitement in every standing-up hair.

There's nothing like it. She's happy, she's complete. She's invincible.

So why does her face look dead whenever she sees it in the mirror? Why are there rings under her eyes? And more than that; purple patches, fading but there. She's tried to cover them, but concealer isn't enough. And today, she needs to be on her game. Mags is depending on her. She takes a huge gulp of coffee and welcomes the caffeine hit.

One more game, she thinks. *One more can't hurt.* But when she tries to load the app, it crashes and then disappears from the screen, and she thinks her heart will stop.

13

NOW

Monday morning, and Facebook is still down. Maggie has no timeline, so she tries Twitter. Same there. Blank. She presses the button to her home screen, and the icons are flickering like her phone is under water. She shakes it and it goes blank.

'Fuck my life!' she says, throwing the phone towards the end of the bed.

She floats downstairs in a haze of last night's red wine, which she'd drunk copiously after chatting to Franny whilst trying to check social media. Her head is buzzing with the start of a headache, so she finds the aspirin and glugs a whole two-pint measuring jug of water.

Her iPad is where she left it at dinner, propped up on its stand on the table. There's a gravy stain on the screen, so she wipes it away with a wet finger that she licks after. The shock of salty beef flavour at such early hour causes her stomach to clutch itself violently, and she just makes it to the sink in time to eject the two pints of water. The tablets come with it.

'Fucking eejit!' she berates herself as she hangs on to the kitchen worktop for a minute, waiting for her world to right itself.

Upstairs, the bear is moving about. She can hear its huge paws padding across the carpet of her bedroom. It's trying to be quiet, but she can almost *feel* its movement; every step it takes is landing on her chest, threatening to stop her heart.

She can't deal with it today.

She opens the fridge. There is a bottle of Veuve Clicquot nestling in the door that she's saving until she's sealed the deal at work. It's for later. It's to celebrate. She and Franny plan to open it and pat each other on the back for another great client in the bag.

No one drinks champagne first thing in the morning.

She pulls out the bottle, removes the foil and untwists the metal in a practised fluid movement. The sound of the cork popping makes her want to weep. She's not sure whether with relief or shame. Maybe both.

After a hefty swig straight from the bottle – she always remembers to leave an air gap and *pour* it in rather than clamp her lips over it which causes an explosion in the mouth and up the nose! – she takes it over to the table and fires up her iPad. She makes mental notes about the running order of the morning. In work early, set up the projector, make sure the presentation works, run through the figures she spent ages putting together with Franny, make coffee, run through everything again.

She remembers Gramps's favourite piece of advice. *Measure twice, cut once.* He was inordinately proud of that, although she always joked it had nothing to do with anything, but she has to admit, it's rubbed off on her and she always checks everything at least twice. It's what makes her a brilliant events coordinator, if she does say so herself.

The iPad screen is blank.

'What the...?' Maggie stares at it. Not a thing on there. No apps or icons; even the background picture has gone. She swipes at the screen, hoping to at least come across her contacts. If she can't phone Franny, she can at least email her.

Nothing.

Irritated, she has to go into the hallway and dig her address book out of her work bag. It's a cumbersome thing because she has so many numbers in it. She wouldn't have it at all if it weren't for her granddad telling her it was best practice.

One day you may need this old-fashioned thing we call paper and ink, Maggie.

The book falls open at the page she's looked at the most, and seeing *Gramps* makes her heart hurt. She takes the landline phone from the hall stand to the kitchen table and gulps more champagne before finding Franny's mobile number. She dials it, but nothing happens. She gets the clicks to say it's calling the number, but there's a silence after, like it's waiting for another digit or something. She tries again. Same thing. She tries Franny's landline.

Franny answers on the first ring. Good girl! She's up.

'Hey, good morning. I'm fine, yes thanks. Is your mobile dead? Mine too. This weird thing that's happening lately is getting worse. I just wanted to check we're all prepared for this morning. Big big day. Have you got the slides all done? Great. See you later. Don't forget I'll be there after my appointment.'

They never say what the appointment is, but Franny knows.

Another large drink of champagne, from a proper flute, and then she pops a spoon into the neck and puts it in the fridge. Two more aspirin – this time she anchors them down with half a slice of toast – a shower, hair straightened with the GHDs, bit of make-up but not too much because that threatens some clients, and then she leaves the house.

It's just a short walk to the tram stop. It's busier than usual, a crowd of about fifteen people wandering around, some of them holding their phones up in the air, like you do when you're trying to get a signal. As her phone is dead, she needs to buy a ticket, so she grabs her card out of her purse and goes to the ticket machine.

There's a line of openly disgruntled people in front of it and one of them, a middle-aged man, is pressing the buttons rapidly like he's playing a fruit machine for the jackpot.

'Is there a problem?' she asks. People are tutting in that passive-aggressive way British people do when they're extremely angry, stressed and inconvenienced.

'Bloody machines are all on the blink,' the man says. 'And all mobile signals appear to be down so we can't find out why.'

'Free rides today then,' a young woman chimes in from the back of the line, and they all stand to wait for the tram.

14

NOW

Maggie has called Franny on her landline, presumably because she can't reach her on her mobile, and it's all Franny can do to keep her mind on the conversation. Something about slides, and being ready, and she says yes but she's not really sure she *is* ready. Something is eating away at her – has been for a while – and she needs to make sense of it. She tells Maggie what she knows she wants to hear, and is satisfied she's convinced her because Maggie hangs up happy.

But Franny is discontented and afraid and...

'Afraid.' She says the word aloud and it bounces off the quietness at such a speed it's like Rafael Nadal has served it at 120 miles an hour. The ricochets are like an assault rifle salvo, and the bullets rip through her, tearing her apart.

She's never admitted it before. She's never said it. She's sat alert and vigilant on the sofa or in bed, waiting for him to come home, waiting for him to come upstairs, waiting for him to do and say whatever he wants to strip her of her humanness and sensitivity. He's numbed her. He's defeated her.

She's only just realised.

All the times she and Mags had talked about *him*, Maggie's

demon and torturer, and what happened all those years ago. He'd been the most frightening man either of them had ever met. And yet, all this time, under their noses, had been another man just as frightening. More frightening actually, because this one got past. This one got in. This one thought he had *rights*.

Why couldn't Steve be like Paul? Paul was a proper man who didn't need anyone else's fear to validate him or make him feel powerful, and that was just what Maggie needed. He walked in and made Maggie's life beautiful. The ugliness Steve has brought to her own is like a sore that just won't heal.

She tries to heal it – has done for a while now – by having a flutter or two on the online games. Even though she knows the odds are against her, and even though she's lost way more money than she's won, nothing will diminish the urge.

She'd first downloaded the app in a fit of boredom on one of the nights Steve had left her alone in the house while he went out drinking with his friends. It wasn't the first time he'd done it, but it was beginning to wear now. It was beginning to leave big old holes in the fabric of their marriage, and elbow patches were definitely needed. So, she sewed on a patch of online roulette and *Twenty-One* and it brought her something she hadn't had for a long time: excitement, hope, something to look forward to.

She thought she was just fed up. Sad. Lonely. But now she knows it's different, it's more. She can't deny the physical stuff. She can't keep hiding that. Now her app, her crutch, has failed her, she can't hide the misery of her life behind the thrill of gambling. She can't ignore the marks, the aches and pains, the bruises of her life any longer.

These last few days, with the strange happenings, and phones and computers breaking down, Franny has been feeling exposed again, and the icy wind is cutting through her, bringing the fear back with a vengeance.

She wishes she could talk to Maggie, but doesn't know how.

15

THEN

She's waiting for her phone to buzz. Last night, at her door, Paul had taken it from her, tapped in his own number, and taken hers. He said he'd text her. She's stared at the bloody screen so long today she wonders if he put a fake number in.

She's only had this iPhone for a couple of months and doesn't really know how it works. Franny told her they needed one of the new Apple phones that were all the rage, but it's much more complicated than her Motorola flip phone. She sees people in the pub, tapping out text messages with lightning thumbs, and she wonders what school people went to to learn all this stuff so quickly.

To pass the time she watches a bit of Saturday morning TV, but the programme, TMI – which in her opinion stands for The Minimum Intelligence – drives her mad after about ten minutes and she turns the telly off.

She can't remember the last time she felt so nervous waiting for someone to call or text her. She's not been out anywhere other than The Cage with Franny for a long time, and the men in there are usually either married – which doesn't stop them from actually wanting to take her out, but she always says no –

or a little strange. And Maggie's well aware that 'strange' is a very subjective opinion to have about someone's personality. She thinks she's strange herself, so has a high tolerance level for people who live outside society's norms. But with men, she classes strange as not being emotionally present; not being in tune with others.

Aside from her granddad, who she didn't live with so didn't see day to day, the best example of a husband she'd ever known was her father, although she didn't have him for very long before he died. As a child observing her parents together, she'd always been struck by how respectful and considerate her dad was. At the time, she didn't have the words to describe it, but she saw with her own eyes how happy her mum always was, how lit up. There was always a lot of singing, and dancing around the kitchen. And laughter; so much of that, all the time.

Every Friday her dad would bring her mum flowers, and every Saturday and Sunday he'd do all the housework and cooking, and not let her mum lift a finger. He'd make pies and cut leaf shapes out to decorate them, and he had a way of making every surface in the house shine, and the whole place smell so good. Maggie used to think it was his beauty that made all that so, and she still does.

And, he'd say to Maggie all the time, as he stood there with a flowery apron on, that if someone ever told her it wasn't manly to wear a flowery apron and that doing cooking and cleaning was woman's work, then she was to run a mile from him.

'Being a man is simple,' he told her. 'All you have to do is prove you believe the truth – that men and women are equal. Full stop. Remember that, my darling. No man should ever try to be better than you, because he's not. He'll be wasting his time.'

She never really understood the things her dad told her back then. She's learned them since. She's come across men who want to dominate, to overpower, to destroy.

She even let one do it. But she's trying, she really is, to make that right. She wants to find a man just like her father, but she's not sure he even exists.

Her phone buzzes, making her jump. She keeps forgetting to change the notification sound and volume, and its three beeps are extremely loud in her quiet living room.

Suddenly, her heart is pounding in her ears, and she feels faint. Should she trust Paul? Should she give him a chance? She wants to, more than anything. Last night he'd driven her home. She'd been really drunk but he'd not laid a hand on her; had kept her safe. The last person who'd always made sure she was safe was her father.

The message on the screen is from *Hunk from the Cage* and she laughs out loud because she hadn't seen what name he'd put in when he added himself to her contacts.

The text message reads:

> Permission requested to take subject away from bodyguard for one evening. Proposed location: Don Giovanni, Oxford Street. Proposed date and time: Friday 8pm. Dress code: Casual, with consideration that some people only own one jacket. RSVP.

She RSVPs, her hands shaking so much it takes her almost a minute to type:

> Permission granted. Bodyguard told to stand down and take a chill pill. Suggest meeting in Odder on Oxford Road before meal. 7pm? Great vibe. Can you still say 'vibe'?

16

THEN

Franny took Scafell Pike, and what happened after as a result, badly, but she kept it to herself. Of course, Maggie had it worse, but she can't help feeling she let her down by allowing it to happen. Maggie kept on saying to her, there was no way she could've stopped it, no way of knowing it was going to happen. But Franny regrets, with every cell of her body, her negligence. Her stupidity. Her selfishness.

There are nights she wakes up thinking she's in the tent next to Maggie, and she finds herself thrashing in sweat-drenched bedclothes at the memory of it. They were supposed to share but had fallen out over something Maggie had claimed had happened in the churchyard earlier in the day. Franny didn't believe her and she'd left Maggie to sleep alone while she dragged her sleeping bag into Tracey Thornton and Carole Cassidy's tent. It had been a squeeze and Franny hadn't been able to sleep because of Carole's terrible snoring. Many times, during the night, she'd thought about moving out and going back, but she'd not wanted to wake anyone.

If only she had gone back. Before it had been too late.

She's vowed to herself, and to Maggie, that she'll never let anyone hurt her again; that she'll always protect her, no matter what. And she's kept that promise. She always vets her boyfriends, checks them out, does a lot of digging around to see if she can find any dirt on them. She likes to think she's saved her from a lot of heartache. Not that Maggie is overly interested in boys, not after what happened with Charlie.

'Without him, I don't really care about anything,' she often says. And that's pretty much the truth. She doesn't have many boyfriends. As they got older and left school, she maybe had one or two, but no one ever stuck.

Not until now. Until Paul.

Franny can't wait to find out what the crack is after last night, so she phones Maggie and can tell right away that she's smitten.

'Did he get you home okay? Was he a gentleman?' she asks. 'Be honest, because I'll know by your voice.'

Maggie bursts out laughing. 'Oh, Fran, you are funny. You sound like an old nun or something. Of course he got me home safely, and everything was fine. I'm still alive.'

'Don't joke about stuff like that! All kinds of things happen.'

'I'm fine, I promise. He kissed me on the cheek and left.'

'Yeah, I know. I followed you.'

'What!' Maggie can't help laughing out loud, and she knows Franny isn't joking, because it's totally something she'd do. 'You're so sneaky. I never saw.'

'That's the point. You weren't supposed to. You know I was a ninja in another life.'

'You didn't see him kiss me though.'

'No, but I saw how long he was at your flat and know he left you at the door.'

'Mmm... yes, he did.'

'You sound disappointed,' Franny says.

'I kind of was,' Maggie admits. 'But... I'm seeing him later. He wants to take me to dinner, but I thought we could meet at Odder first, have a few drinks. Will you come? For the drinks, I mean, not the dinner. You can piss off then.'

'Charming.'

17

NOW

The tram is buzzing with a strange noise. It doesn't sound like it usually does; it's not normal.

Maggie realises what it is: conversation. She's never heard it before on her run to work. Usually, people are wired into their MP3 players, or their phones, scrolling through social media for validation and irritation, but today the air is filled with a hum that's part puzzlement, part curiosity.

The sun is streaming in through the windows, and she tilts her face to feel it. The warmth is like a caress and makes her think, briefly, of her mother. She used to be a major giver of cuddles and kisses, but hasn't been so for a long time now.

Maggie doesn't like the way her thoughts are heading. Why, on this important day, does she have to think of her mother? She doesn't approve of her work. She doesn't like her friends. She doesn't relish the fact her daughter is seeing a psychiatrist. Maggie has tried to explain to her that it's a therapist, not a psychiatrist, and that there's a big difference – although she doesn't really know herself what that is. But her mother is blinkered, and only sees her daughter as seeing a head shrink. And she feels ashamed of that, Maggie knows it.

Damn, she doesn't want this. Today is already stressful enough. She doesn't want to continue thinking of the woman who treated her like she did. She doesn't want to think about the woman who took away everything she had.

She just wants to get to her appointment, get that out of the way, and then concentrate on the presentation. Work is the only thing that keeps her sane – or at least slightly less crazy.

But... the tram is now doing a weird vibrating thing and the people standing and holding on to straps and poles are jiggling around in a strange way.

What now? Maggie thinks, as the tram lurches to a stop halfway between St Peter's Square and Piccadilly Gardens. She looks at her watch. Just ten minutes until her appointment, but the driver has got out and is attaching a set of ladders to one of the exits. He's helping people down.

'Shit!' Maggie curses, gathers up her bags, gets off, and starts walking.

As if she'd known Maggie had been thinking about her, her mum decides to call just as she's walking through the gardens. She considers rejecting the call but thinks better of it. She might as well get it over with because she'll never give up.

'Hi, Mum. Can't speak for long. I'm about to go into a meeting. How are you today?'

'My head is hurting, Margaret. And I can't get ITV. I can't miss Corrie.'

She always calls her Margaret these days, says Maggie is for a child and she's a grown woman now. Maggie is convinced she does it to annoy her.

'I showed you how to watch it on your tablet, Mum.'

'Oh, I can't be bothered with that fiddly thing and it's not working. The screen is broken, I think, because all those little things are gone.'

Maggie sighs. 'Okay, Mum, I'll call round after work. Is that okay?'

Although, she's no idea how she's going to help get ITV back, if indeed it is gone. Last time her mum said it had gone, it was just stuck on BBC because she'd lost the remote in a pile of crap building up in her living room. It's like an episode of *Hoarders* in her house, and Maggie hates going there. She can see the unravelling of her mum's mind represented in the piles of magazines, newspaper, food containers and random objects from her past.

She throws nothing away, which Maggie finds irritating, because she threw *her* away. Or rather, she threw away something, someone, so precious to Maggie, she still can't think about it without becoming undone.

So, she stifles it.

'I suppose it'll have to be okay,' her mum says, and Maggie hangs up without saying another word.

She'll tell her later it was the phone cutting out.

18

NOW

Simon Goodwin is pissed off. His phone is playing up and he can't access his music drive. Also, he's expecting an important email, and every time he tries to open the app, it comes up blank. On the news they said it's most likely to be temporary, but "most likely" isn't good enough for him. When he's stressed, he needs music. He needs those rock gods, Rainbow. He needs Joe Lynn Turner's voice to make everything okay.

All his mates think he's mad for listening to "rock dinosaurs" when there's so much banging music around these days. He agrees about the music; he loves Wolf Alice and Joy Division, but has to balance the modern stuff with Rainbow, Donovan and Johnny Cash. All this he blames on his mum and dad, although it can't be in his blood because he's adopted. But their tastes rubbed off on him and he loves that he has this mix in his heart and soul.

One of his earliest memories is of a picnic at Heaton Park, on a day when everything was bathed in gorgeous sunshine. He was sitting on a blanket – a huge blue and red tartan one – and his mum was unpacking plates, cups and napkins. While she served up the sandwiches and pork pies, his dad was fiddling with the knobs on his giant cassette player, whistling tunes even before he put them in the tape deck. That day it was all about Mario Lanza, the American tenor. Their house had always been filled with him, either on the record player or the films his mum watched. His voice was velvet, it was treacle. It was his childhood.

So now, music is important to him and he's so grateful he got that grounding and received the majorly important gift of being a real music lover. To him, that means appreciating music for itself, and not for how popular or "trendy" something is. It's all about emotion and feeling something in your bones and the very heart of you. So, he's known as someone with eclectic tastes, and sometimes he gets ribbed mercilessly for it. But he doesn't care. It's helped him set up the coolest – in his opinion – record and music shop in the centre of Manchester, which is like earning money for just breathing!

Today, though, he can't play anything.

At Droylsden, his best friend, Archie Maxwell, gets on the tram, and they bump fists.

'Sup, dude,' Archie says. 'You look like you just ate a mouldy pie.'

Simon laughs. 'I'd prefer that to discovering my whole music library can't be opened. If I've lost everything...'

'Oh yeah, the pulses, dude. Are we being invaded?'

'I doubt it, but whatever it is, I hope it doesn't last long because I can't handle it. Even streaming isn't working right now. I swear, I'm going mad!'

The tram trundles along towards the town centre, and Simon keeps on stealing glances at his phone, hoping it's going to start working again very soon.

'You on a promise or something, dude?' Archie asks. "What are you waiting for? You know the phones aren't working.'

'I'm waiting for an email. It's really important.'

'Ah, the one you're keeping from your mum?'

'Yeah, that's the one. Mum's literally the word. Okay?'

Archie zips up his lips, locks them, and throws the key over his shoulder.

19

NOW

Maggie has a strained relationship with her mother. They dance around each other, they hide, they say things they don't mean, and the things they mean, they keep inside. Every time she phones, the tension between them gets dredged to the surface and it's excruciating. Exhausting.

When Maggie's dad died, they were close for a few years. They only had each other, and the shared bond of loving the same man and then losing him kept them friends for a while.

They'd spend entire evenings looking at photos of him before he got ill, talking about the evenings they used to spend playing board games like Cluedo and Monopoly, which her dad always cheated at. He never let anyone else be the banker and they soon discovered why; he was palming fifties like they were going out of fashion.

They'd bond over these reminiscences, and the memories were lovely and joyous, so they could push away the grief a little. It hid behind their plates of cakes, behind their teapot and teacups, behind their smiles and their mummy-daughter Disney movie nights with popcorn and lemonade. But soon, the good memories ran out, like a film reel reaching the end of the spool, and the positive B-movie ended and the bad-memory main feature started, and it was these memories that changed everything. They were crippling.

At first his decline had been slow and gradual, so much so, Maggie started to believe that either he was lying to her about his illness, or he was mistaken. She couldn't imagine the former to be true, so she began to tell herself the doctors had got it wrong. In the past, whenever her mum had invited her friends round to drink tea and talk about other mums they knew, they'd often talk about who was ill, and one of the things she always heard was that doctors didn't know what they were talking about. So, Maggie clung on to this; let it push away her fear.

When he first went for his rounds of treatment, he'd come back looking exactly the same as when he left the house. Maggie had observed him, coming through the door on his return from the hospital. He'd come in as normal, thrown his coat and hat onto the peg and shouted 'Tea, woman!' in that jokey way he had.

It was when he stopped that that Maggie's heart tightened. He started to come in stooped, limping and holding his body as if there was something terrible nesting inside it. And instead of shouting for tea he'd take to his bed and sleep for hours.

And, as he'd told her he would, he started to lose his hair. He became an old dad, way before she had the chance to grow old with him.

When he got too weak to sit in his armchair anymore, he moved into a bed her mother brought downstairs. He said he didn't want to be lying all alone like a dying patient upstairs; he'd rather do it downstairs. That he tried to joke about it was excruciating to Maggie, because she actually found it funny, and when she laughed her heart hurt so much she thought she'd be the one to die. He'd always been able to make her laugh, and that shared humour they had would die with him. It was unbearable.

Because her mother also found those secondary memories traumatic, they drifted apart. Neither of them wanted to get together anymore to share them. They'd used up all the good times they recalled, and all they could remember was pain.

It's all they can remember still.

When they meet now, or talk on the phone, her mum always says her dad would be appalled that she puts her work before her family, before making her mother happy. Where's the husband? Where are the children?

Maggie wants to tell her it doesn't matter because he's dead and he's not watching, and children aren't all they're cracked up to be because they just end up getting screwed up and fall out with their families, and end up having to pay a fortune for therapy.

It's a vicious circle that's been expanding ever since her trip to Scafell Pike.

Ever since she tried to tell her.

20

THEN

Maggie can't eat. She's at the table staring at a plate of scrambled eggs, and her stomach is turning over and over like she's on the Big Dipper, only she's never been on the Big Dipper, but Franny says her brother told her it was great. Franny and Maggie have only been on the Mouse and the Grand National, and even those made Maggie's stomach turn. Like it's turning now.

She has something to tell her mum, and the words are stuck in her throat like when bread swells up after you've tried to swallow a big lump of it along with a big glug of milk. Once, at school, they'd been given bread and butter pudding, made by the permanently angry dinner lady who had nicotine-stained fingers, and it had been so dense Maggie hadn't been able to swallow it. She'd had to cough it up into her serviette, had hidden it in her school bag, and disposed of it in the bin outside the newsagent on the way home.

It had been like a huge lump of alien matter, and that's what she felt like she had in her throat now.

'What's up? You not hungry?' her mother asks. She puts her hand on Maggie's forehead and frowns as if she can't decide whether she has a temperature or not. 'It's not like you, and you need your breakfast. It's the most important meal of the day.'

Her mum's mothering instinct has changed lately. She used to show it with lots of cuddles and laughter. Ever since her dad died, it's transformed into offering all the other mothering things, like cooking and cleaning, and making sure all Maggie's clothes are clean and pressed and the house and their tiny family life ticks over like clockwork. But there's never any emotion anymore. She tells Maggie when and what to eat, and seems concerned about her health, but it's perfunctory.

'I feel a little sick,' Maggie says. 'I have to tell you something. It's about Mr Roberts.'

'What about Mr Roberts?' Her mum is scrubbing the stove top to remove some splashes of egg. She's not looking at Maggie.

'When I was camping...' She wished her mum would stop scrubbing, would turn around. '...he came into my tent.'

'Came into your tent? He was inspecting it, I imagine.'

'No, he wasn't inspecting it. It was late at night and...'

'Margaret, stop this nonsense.' Her mum throws her dishcloth into the sink. 'You've always been a bit of a dreamer – I blame your father – but it's not nice to make up stories about people. You could get Mr Roberts into trouble. He's a nice man. Now get on with your breakfast. You have to eat all your egg.'

Maggie eats all her egg, but ten minutes later she throws it up in the outside loo.

21

THEN

Cynthia Milburn has hair like a horse's mane. It's the thing about her that gives her her superpower. Every night she brushes it one hundred times, like all the magazines say you must. She imagines herself as the heroine in every romantic film, and as she grows from a girl to a young woman, the desire to find a man who'll sweep her off her feet and carry her away on a white stallion becomes stronger and stronger. She can picture the scene: him dressed in leather trousers and a nice shirt, with his muscles on show and his jet-black locks all wavy and masculine, and her on the back, in a long gown with her hair streaming behind and matching the length of the horse's tail, which will be the same chestnut brown.

When she meets her prince for real, he's a goofball with medium-length mousy hair he has to keep sweeping back from his face, and no discernible muscles. He makes her laugh a lot, so she forgives him his shortcomings. He's kind and gentle, and he does open doors for her, but tells her she has to do it for him when the opportunity arises.

They have a daughter together and they raise her at odds with each other, but somehow it works. Maggie does as Cynthia tells her most of the time on matters of good manners and decency, but veers towards her father on what Charles calls the fundamentals of life – like the so-called sexual revolution, and whether a woman should travel alone without a man to protect her, or go into a restaurant or other public place on her own. Cynthia finds it all far too progressive, but she humours the man she worships, and the daughter she adores.

Maggie looks like her father. Same mousy-brown hair which will soon become a honey-gold, same blue eyes that catch light like multi-faceted sapphires, same upturned lips that give the impression they're always smiling, no matter what happens.

When Maggie is still quite young, Charles is diagnosed with bowel cancer, and during his year-long fight, Cynthia's hair turns almost white, and Charles's falls out completely. There doesn't seem much to smile about in the Milburn household, but Charles' and Maggie's upturned mouths carry the house on a cloud of jokes and positivity.

After her husband's death, Cynthia cuts her white hair short; so short she never really has to comb it again.

22

NOW

She has to check to make sure he's still alive.

Maggie has been in his office for ten minutes, has helped herself to coffee as instructed, sat down on his couch and, after that, a silence has dropped like a curtain and shows no signs of lifting. Taylor Clarke is sitting in his oversized leather armchair, his grey-slacked legs crossed right over left, and in his lap is a notebook with a swirly Celtic design on the cover. He's staring ahead, at a point just above Maggie's shoulder.

From her very first meeting with him she knew he was going to irritate her. She hadn't even wanted to meet him in the first place, but Franny had insisted because she was worried about her. Apparently, her cousin had 'come on in leaps and bounds' after seeing him for eighteen months. She'd given Maggie his card, which was printed on lilac coloured paper and had *Taylor Clarke – Therapist* in a funny scrolling script.

'But I'm okay, Franny,' she'd insisted, ignoring that look on Franny's face. What Maggie called her 'tickling the tummy of a puppy dog' face... all scrunched up and overly cutesy and twee, and so bloody condescending. In her heart, though, she knows Franny loves her and is worried, but she's coped with this for the best part of twenty-four years and she's still alive, isn't she? Although, she's lost count of the days she vomits before work, or grapples with that bloody bear in the morning when she gets out of bed.

The card irritates Maggie too. The colour mostly, and there's a tiny, almost imperceptible space in the word therapist and all she can see whenever she looks at the card is *Taylor Clarke – The rapist* and it always makes her want to scream.

Maggie can't imagine anything worse than having to unload her private thoughts to someone for eighteen months, but she's stuck with him now. The rapist. The man who wears woollen cardigans with leather elbow patches, who scratches himself far too often, and who wears that aftershave; the one that brings something more than a smell. The one that brings pictures of that face scorched red by the mountain sun, and heat of breath stinking of beer and fags.

'So,' he says, breaking the silence and the noise of Maggie's thoughts, and she can't imagine ever telling him about the things she's thinking.

Instead, she lies. She'll always lie, because of the only three men in her life she trusts, one died when she was seven, one is going to die soon and one she made a huge mess of things with – and that's about as much as she can take of pain, thanks all the same.

'So...' She searches for something to say, like she always does. Some frippery, some shallow chit-chat that will skate around the truth and the pain and triple salchow its way into quiet demise. Without challenge. Without questions.

'Franny and I have this big job on at the moment. So much work, we don't have time for anything else. Very prestigious client – a local businessman with a huge extended family. He's paying for weddings for all five of his nieces, and wants to do them all separately, which is a dream for us. Most multiple weddings are done on the same day, you know, people sharing the spotlight and therefore all the cost. But he wants five separate dos and frankly, that's going to be amazing for us. Five weddings, five times the cost.'

She realises she's rambling and stops, looks at her fingernails. When she looks up, the rapist is staring at her quietly, with his hands joined and his two index fingers making a steeple that he rests the apex of on his lips. He's nodding lightly and making *hmm, hmm* noises.

It unnerves Maggie.

'So anyway, we have to impress him, and... what?' Irritated now, his stare, his silence, the bloody steeple of his fingers.

'When are you going to start talking to me, Maggie?'

23

NOW

Everything is in a locked metal box, but she daren't open it. If she does, all those things she secured inside there – the sounds, the smells, the sensations – will all come jumping out, like some malevolent jack-in-the-box.

Along with the St Christopher on a silver chain she'd received at her communion and worn all through school and into adulthood would come the memory of her dad, and the love she had for him that was wrenched away so suddenly. The St Christopher represents the expectations and belief he had in her that she thinks she didn't fulfil.

Along with the charcoal rubbing of a gravestone in the Cumbrian churchyard would come the memory of the thighs pressed too close behind her when no one was looking, and the weight that had pressed down later that night in her sleeping bag, numbing her body and making it immobile.

Along with the tin that contained the faintest trace of aniseed smell would come the memory of the strangest bus journey home ever, when she'd held everything inside her, like she was a pressure cooker with a stuck lid.

And the bracelet. Talking about that would just blow her world completely apart.

So, the box lives in her closet, on a top shelf, and in front of it is a row of shoes she never wears, so never has to move. The rapist talks like it's the easiest thing in the world to bring that box down from its shelf and open it. It's all right for him, with his leather patches and his leather shoes and his gentleman's club fucking attitude, and the damn notebook into which he's probably just doodling and pretending he's writing down important things.

'Open the box, Maggie.'

Maggie jumps in her seat. Is he reading her mind? How does he know about the box? And then she remembers; she told him about it a few weeks ago when she'd been feeling in a particularly sharing mood. Sometimes that happens. Sometimes she thinks there's a chink of light, like through a door being cranked ever-so-slowly open. And when that happens, if she tugs it fully open and steps through, she believes she can bask in the glow of light and feel normal. Even if only for a moment.

She wants to tell him – about the St Christopher, the charcoal rubbing, the tin of aniseed sweets, and the bracelet – maybe. She wants to throw each item at him and have him catch them, and show her they're just things. That they can put them back in the box and throw it away.

But she can't. Not yet. Still not yet.

'I think our hour is up,' she says, although there are still ten minutes left.

24

THEN

Odder, on Oxford Road, lives up to its name. Colourful, vibrant, covered in clocks and giant lizards, it has two vibes going on at once. Chilled out downstairs so people can meet for a drink after work or uni and let the strains of the day drift away with every drink, and pulsing and dancey upstairs in the live music section.

Maggie and Franny have been coming here since it opened and their faces, among many others, are as much a part of the decor as the strange artefacts and bright fittings. Although they remain loyal to The Cage as their local, this place serves all their weekend raving needs. Great wine and cocktails, fabulous networking and socialising, and then later, if they want it, brilliant music and dancing upstairs.

It's six thirty, and they've arrived early to settle their nerves before meeting Paul. He's been given strict instructions not to get there before seven. He laughed when receiving the order, but agreed. Maggie is shaking a little, and this annoys her; it amuses Franny though.

'God, I've never seen you like this,' Franny says, as she waves at the bartender. She holds up two fingers and he pours them two glasses of rosé – their 'starting drink of choice'.

'So, Mags,' Franny says. 'What's the plan? Thanks, Mike.'

'There's no plan. Plans are for buildings. I operate on a strictly spontaneous level.'

'Yeah, you say that, but I'm willing to bet a month's salary that you've shaved your legs and trimmed your garden, and... that you're wearing new underwear.'

At the word 'garden' Maggie laughs into her drink, sending wine shooting out of the glass.

'Fran!' But she's right. Everything is in good order below her waist. At least, she thinks it's in good order, but she's never been good at stuff like that.

When Paul arrives, Maggie has one of those moments that only happen once in a while – at least for her. As he walks through the door, bringing with him a slant of evening sunlight that lights up the bar where she and Franny are standing so it seems like a spotlight heralding his arrival, she feels her stomach twist into a massive knot. Not an unpleasant feeling. She'd almost forgotten his floppy hair, the deep wells of his eyes, the half-smile on his lips.

'So, you weren't joking about the jacket,' she says. She can't stop smiling. She feels as though her mouth isn't her own, that someone else is controlling it. 'Do I need to take you shopping?'

'Only if that's what makes you happy,' Paul says. He comes closer to Maggie and plants a kiss on her cheek. She instantly remembers the sensations from last time; the softness but firmness of his lips, the slight graze of the stubble he wears, which she finds incredibly sexy, the gentle pop of air in the gesture, and the flinch-and-you'll-miss-it warmth of his breath as he starts to move away. She has a sudden urge to grab his arm, pull him in, feel those lips on hers.

But she stifles it.

There's someone standing behind him, eclipsed by his height. Suddenly he pops his head around. A pleasant, handsome face.

'Oh, this is Steve,' Paul says. 'He's my safety net. If things go well, he'll leave me when we go for dinner. If not, he's going to fake a heart attack so I "have to take him to the hospital".' He does air quotes at the last bit. 'Steve, meet Maggie. And the beauty beside her is the lovely Franny. She's the one I warned you about. Has a black belt in ju-jitsu and don't-take-no-shit-su.'

'Ladies,' Steve says, and shakes hands with them both; lingers a beat on Franny, locks eyes with her.

And so it begins. And it feels just like that to Maggie. A beginning. But also, the ending of so much bad stuff. She can feel it.

Franny collars her in the loos, just before she's about to leave with Paul for dinner.

'Oh, Mags, I love him so much! He's going to be so good to you.' She hugs Maggie. 'Oh, and kudos for Steve, don't you think? He's a doll and I can't wait to play with him.'

A beginning for Franny too. Things couldn't look any better.

25

NOW

After speaking to her therapist, Maggie calls into a coffee shop on Piccadilly Place for a flat white and a touch of sanity. She takes it out to drink in the square. There's a new installation of giant lamps and she sits under a massive Anglepoise to sip and compose herself before heading to the office. It's warm, and the sun is poking its face down into the square with a morning smile. Around her, Manchester is alive with people coming and going. It always amazes Maggie that so many people are out and about during the day. People are supposed to be at work. But everyone has something unique to do. Everyone apparently has a purpose.

She wishes *her* purpose was to be better at talking to her therapist. This morning is perfect in that she's up, she's on her way to work, she has a cup of joe, and all should be right in the world. Her business is really successful after just three years, and she couldn't have a better partner in Franny. She wishes she didn't have so much baggage and could just enjoy it.

When she and Franny had that lightbulb moment, about going into business together, over drinks at her flat, it was such a defining moment. Neither of them could explain why they hadn't thought of it before. They'd actually spent many drunken hours, in the pub or at each other's place, talking about how great they'd be at event planning, because they were both so good at organising everyone's lives. Their friends came to them for advice about everything: shopping, careers, boyfriends. Some of them had got married or had baby showers. And Maggie and Franny were superb at arranging them. So why not do it for a living?

It had been hard getting financing, but in the end they'd managed with a small business loan and a generous dose of help from Maggie's granddad – which he insisted he didn't want paying back – and Milburn Jones Events was launched. They'd eventually been able to move out of their respective shitty flats and into better places. Franny has a modest home in Eccles and Maggie a townhouse on Merchants Quay. They are truly living the dream. On the outside at least.

But why is everything still so damned hard? Why can't she talk about any of the things with her therapist? She knows it'll help.

But she also knows it will hurt. Opening that box... taking out those hidden and secret things, one by one. It'll break her open too.

26

THEN

Maggie knows she looks beautiful, like a princess. She can see it in her dad's expression. It looks like he's going to cry, but he'll say he has something in his eye. He always says this when they're watching old films on the telly and it gets to the end where the man gets the girl, or someone dies. Her mum always elbows him gently in his side and calls him a soppy apeth and they all have a good giggle at him. In reality, he doesn't mind being seen to cry. He can't do. He does it too much. And he always says there's nothing wrong with displaying emotion, that keeping it in is what makes people hard and damaged.

'You look so lovely, Maggie,' he says in a voice thick as treacle. Maggie whirls around in her white Communion dress. It's short, just above the knee. Her veil is also short. She knows most of the other girls have gone for midi length, but she prefers this. Her shoes are the shiniest of shiny patent leather T-bars in the brightest white. She feels like someone from a fairy tale and tells her dad this.

'You look like a princess, darling,' he agrees. 'But you know I'd love you even if you were Cinderella before her transformation, don't you?'

'I know, Daddy.' He's always telling her this. That she's beautiful no matter what. No matter what she looks like, or what she's doing, or what she chooses to do in the future. That beauty comes from inside, from what's in her heart. Not from anything happening to her in life, unless she dictates it.

'Wherever you choose to go in life, you know it'll always be the right decision as long as it makes you happy and you don't hurt anyone else to reach your destination.'

Maggie loves her father so much but she's seven, and she can't see the destination he's talking about. She goes to school and church, and sometimes to Frances Jones's house for tea. But he keeps telling her: 'Go wherever you want to. Travel anywhere, everywhere. Experience everything.'

Today, he has something in a small box, and as he watches her twirling around, he hugs it to his chest with two hands. It catches Maggie's eye – the red velvet. She stops whirling.

'What's that, Daddy?' she asks, her eyes wide.

'Ah, it's for you, my dearest traveller,' he says and holds it out. Maggie is breathless from the spinning, and from excitement that's raining little hammer blows inside her ribcage. She takes the box.

Inside, nestled on a crumpled bed of red satin, is a necklace made of silver. On the chain is a small heart-shaped medal with an engraved picture of a man with a walking stick, carrying a baby on his shoulders.

'It's for strength and protection, wherever you go. The man is St Christopher. He carried a child across a river, not realising it was baby Jesus.'

'Wow, that's cool,' Maggie says. 'Why is it in the shape of a heart?'

'Because whenever you wear it, it means our hearts are next to each other, and I'll always be with you.'

But he's not always with her. One year later he's dead. And even if he had been alive, he wouldn't be there to protect her on the trip to the Lake District.

Not him, not St Christopher, not even God. And no matter how close the silver heart lay to hers, it still happened.

27

THEN

Maggie travelled. Just as her father always wanted her to. With that St Christopher, he was giving her the gift of freedom, or so he thought at the time. But travelling isn't always about freedom, as Maggie discovered. Often it's about prison, and trying to escape it. If you travel with a talisman around your neck that was given to you with so much hope, it can become a heavy millstone, a hindrance.

Maggie so wanted to live the life her father wanted for her, but the pressure was too much. After his death, and the thing, and all that came after the thing, as soon as she was old enough, she flew. As far as she could and for as long as she could.

At first, being a British traveller, especially a female alone, was exciting, but she soon realised her temperament wasn't suited to such a hippy-esque lifestyle. When it became clear that she wasn't the kind of free spirit who wanted to conquer her sexual self, and that indeed she wanted to remain celibate, everything lost its lustre. Being attracted to dark, sexy men was no use when everything stopped short of that act. It was frustrating for her, and the men, and sometimes dangerous.

She had a relationship with a Greek waiter named Andros

in Corfu, which she only consummated at the last moment after five weeks of pestering from him. It wasn't a good experience, and they'd both been so drunk she wasn't even sure they did it properly.

Sitting on Greek beaches alone a la Shirley Valentine, talking to a rock, wasn't her thing, she discovered, so she came home.

She missed her grandparents, missed Franny, missed Manchester. It was time to settle and make her mark. Make her dad proud.

The first thing she did on returning, apart from vowing never to travel again, was put the St Christopher in her metal memories box, under lock and key. It wasn't working, it wasn't for her.

So, she kept it with all the other things she didn't want to see ever again.

28

NOW

'He'll be here at twelve and we don't have a bloody presentation! What are we going to do?'

They've been working on this wedding account for months and they need to present it to Mr Khan in a professional, polished way so he'll fall in love with all their ideas and suggestions and hand over the best part of £25,000. Franny is waggling cables at the back of the computer like that will do any good.

'Franny, you're stressing me out. I don't think it has anything to do with the cables. We need to think.'

Franny can't think. There's a tiny pinprick of pain behind her right eyeball and she's terrified it'll bloom into something. She's drunk a whole five hundred millilitre bottle of water and is on her second, trying to dilute the booze from last night, and now she's feeling queasy on top of it. She's terrified she'll let Maggie down.

'We could do with your Steve here,' Maggie says. 'He'd know what to do.'

'He's on a big job today. He left early and I'm not sure when he'll be back.'

The lie is easy. She can't bring herself to tell Maggie the truth. She's not sure she even knows what that is herself. She could get him to help if she wanted to. He's always had a thing for Maggie; for anyone who isn't *her*, really. But she doesn't want him here.

'Everything all right with you two?' Maggie asks.

'Fine, yes. We're fine,' Franny replies, but she can't look at her.

Fine has so many different definitions. It can mean attractive or impressive, or of very high quality.

But it also means thin or narrow. Delicate. Liable to break. Franny doesn't dare risk the snap by talking about it now. It's too close to the presentation. She needs to keep her focus.

29

NOW

Experts at Apple, Microsoft, Google and other major tech companies are today scratching their heads at a failure in their systems they are finding hard to explain.

It appears many consumers are reporting incidents of major data loss, with their social media accounts, file storage and hard drives all being wiped intermittently and, in some cases, completely.

Spokespersons from all the big names are asking their customers not to worry and assuring them the issue will be investigated and everything done to rectify the problem.

Early speculation suggests the problem may have been caused by voltage spikes which can occur for any of several reasons, including lightning strikes and electromagnetic pulses. However, experts say it's far too early to speculate about what could be as innocuous as a series of short circuits, which can be easily rectified.

More news as we get it, but in the meantime, people are being urged not to panic.

30

NOW

After all the speculation about what the technology glitches are, the bulletin from BBC News provides a little more information but doesn't fill Maggie and Franny with much confidence. However, they manage to get the cables jiggled, or maybe it's a coincidence, but after half an hour, the iMac fires up and the projector has something to project at last. Maggie almost collapses onto the floor at the relief of it. Franny appears to have the shakes and is as white as a sheet. But the main thing is, they're up and running.

Maggie busies herself flicking one last time through the slides. She giggles at the fact they are using slides for this presentation, because she and Franny always used to laugh when they had team meetings in their previous jobs and middle management losers rolled out the slides and the mouse pointer. Talking about those people in the pub was a major highlight of their week.

'God, what sad sacks,' they'd say over cocktails or pints of beer. 'Let's shoot each other if we ever get to that stage.'

Maggie looks at Franny now and nods towards the screen,

puts two fingers to her temple and pulls her thumb trigger. She laughs but Franny doesn't.

'You okay, Fran?' she asks, surprised she hasn't got the reference.

'Yeah, I'm just tired.' Franny tries a weak smile. 'And duh! Yeah, the PowerPoint, right? Remind me to give you your marching orders from our Cool Girl gang.'

Maggie knows Franny's going through the motions and that there's something lurking just beneath the surface, but she decides to let it go for now. She'll bring it up later.

Mr Khan arrives, punctual as always, at 11.50am and Maggie offers him tea and asks their receptionist, Kelly, to make it for him. She has some special Pakistani chai just for him – aromatic with cardamom, and sweet and milky – and has had Kelly practise it over and over the last few weeks. Soon the room is filled with the scent, and it has the effect of calming Maggie down.

'Eid Mubarak,' she says as she hands him his cup, remembering, and his face lights up.

'Thanks so much, Margaret. Khair Mubarak – thank you for your wishes.' Mr Khan takes the tea from the tray Kelly brought in. There are stem ginger biscuits too, which the lady on the market she got the tea from said would complement the tea perfectly.

'Oh please, call me Maggie. My mum calls me Margaret and I always feel like I'm in trouble when I hear it.'

'Okay, Maggie.' Mr Khan sips his tea and Maggie is pleased to see his eyes narrow with pleasure. 'This is delicious. We are drinking plenty of this at home at the moment. We have lots to celebrate and to thank Allah for. Do you have any cinnamon or turmeric?'

'Er...' Maggie flashes a panicked look at Franny. Franny shrugs as if to say: *Who the hell knew you had to put bloody spice in it?* Mr Khan sees the exchange and bursts out laughing, but kindly.

'Oh please, don't worry. This is lovely just as it is.' He's such a gentleman.

But Maggie feels it; a sense of failure, already, before she's even begun. She takes a deep breath, aware out of the corner of her eye that Franny is doing their secret *calm down, we've got this* signal, which is what they call the *Made-in-Chelsea*-esque hair flick they dreamed up and perfected one night after demolishing two bottles of Prosecco and doing sambuca shots. It's random enough to be unseen by anyone else, but funny enough that after every meeting where they use it, they can laugh about it over drinks and high fives for a job well done.

So, Maggie takes a deep breath as she opens the presentation.

The screen is blank.

31

NOW

A miracle has happened and they've managed to walk Mr Khan through every part of their proposal without the use of modern technology. Luckily, all the price points and details are either in Maggie's head or in her giant notebook, so she's done an admirable job of muddling through it, and she's seen the *Made in Chelsea* hair flick from Franny three times behind Mr Khan's back. Actually, muddling through it would be inaccurate. She's nailed it. She's a pro, she's brilliant at her job, and she knows it.

Before he left, he signed on the dotted line, so Maggie and Franny are now jumping all over the office like lunatics, alarming the young Kelly who, at nineteen, is still a little afraid of her own shadow. However, even she is finding it hard to resist the giddiness and is laughing and clapping at the antics, and saying well done, great job.

When Kelly leaves for lunch, Maggie and Franny grab their own lunches from the fridge, along with a bottle of Veuve Clicquot. It's tempting to go out to eat somewhere fabulous in Spinningfields, but that would lead to too much drinking and Maggie wants to finish some figures for another client.

Maggie wants to talk about how Fran reacted to the mention

of Steve earlier. Truth is, she's noticed something in her friend's attitude and mood for a while and needs to get into it a little.

'How're things at home, Fran?' she asks, and sees a definite squirm deep down in Franny. Her eyes also dart away; Franny does this when she doesn't want to talk about something and is about to lie her arse off.

'Fine.' There's that word again. Pointless word. Fine always means not fine. It should be deleted from the English language.

'Stop with the "everything's fine" bullshit. I know you're not fine. I know you.'

'It's just...' Franny falters, puts her sandwich down without touching it. She picks up her glass and takes a long swig of champagne.

'Just what, Fran? Tell me. Please.' Maggie's voice is barely more than a whisper, her heart pounding in her chest. She can feel something hanging there like a partly severed limb. All of a sudden, the mood in the office has altered from celebratory to one of intense foreboding. She can almost taste it.

Maggie's mobile rings and it makes her jump because of the quiet that's come over the room, and also because it hasn't rung for what seems ages with all the technical problems doing the rounds.

'Shit!' She drops her sandwich and gets her phone out of the bag. It's her gran. Before she answers, she says: 'We *will* have this chat, Fran. Hold those thoughts. Hi, Gran, what's up?'

'Darling, are you at work?'

'Yes, why?" She can hear something in her gran's voice and feels a fear that's far worse than anything worrying about Fran can bring.

'You need to get here, darling. It's time.'

32

THEN

Maggie has had sex once. She's twenty-three, so she knows this is pretty lame. She's seen *Sex and the City*, which frankly scares her, and according to the characters in that, her one-count should be per week, at the very least, not per sexually active career to date at her age.

Of course, her count is really two, but she doesn't ever consider that first one a time. It languishes at the back of her head, and deep deep down in her heart and belly. If it tries to come up, she bashes it down with whatever tools are to hand: food, alcohol, watching TV, or reading books that take her to another place. Being somewhere else is important to her, because staying where she is, in her mind, is... not good. The bear she met as a cub when she was sixteen hasn't left her side and she tires of it sometimes. When she works, it lies low. When she's with Franny and they're laughing at the world, it hides in its lair. When she's in love it stays silent and just watches her life unfold in new and undulating ways; ways filled with butterfly stomach and shaking knees. It watches, but she always knows it's only a matter of time. And it always comes out, bites off the head of any relationship, then lies back down to sleep.

None of her dates make it to the sex stage. She always reaches the same conclusion before too long: they're going too fast and she feels the same fear she always does, at precisely the same point in every relationship she's ever had. She can't even pinpoint or recognise what brings it on, not really. She's not sure if it's a look they get – like they suddenly see her – or the sudden touch of their hand in the cinema or over the table at a restaurant. That touch, that look, shows intimacy, ownership, familiarity. Whatever it is, it kills it all stone dead before she has time to process how she's going to escape. And she runs, up the aisle, out the foyer, or through the tables of dining folk with no cares in the world, and into the wide-open world that for her has always been a challenge because she can't function in it like everyone else.

However, she has a feeling that Paul is different. It seems so clichéd but it's true.

Today, he's taking her to the Manchester Museum of Transport, which Maggie finds hilarious and weirdly romantic, because he's told her his uncle Bob was a bus driver and he was the only man in his dad's imbecile family who ever worked a decent day in his life, and he's also the man who often stepped up when Paul and his mum needed anything when his dad was inside, or when he was outside and knocking seven shades of shite out of his mum.

'Whenever I go and see the old buses, Mags, I see him, in his uniform – he looked so great in it. He'd let me on for free, of course, and sometimes I'd spend whole days with him, escaping everything and travelling the length and breadth of Greater Manchester.

'There was something so great about being involved in his work for a whole day. It captivated me and held my attention without being electronic, or computer based. Imagine being held in thrall by looking outward – out to the world – rather than inward and being swallowed by technology and computer games or TV.'

Maggie loves the image of a young Paul – who in her imagination is wearing short trousers and a school blazer at all times – having the time of his life with his uncle. Loves it because she knows that for most of the time growing up, his life was grim, and scary, and lacking in anything good.

She also loves that despite all the crap, Paul has turned out to be a wonderful human being, and she's fallen hard.

33

THEN

Paul never drinks alcohol. Maggie has offered it to him a couple of times, with dinner or while they're watching a film on the telly because there's nothing she likes more than snuggling up under a blanket with an old weepie, a bowl of popcorn and some wine. But he always declines.

She tells him he could never be anything like his dad, and he asks her how she knows. How does she know? His dad was lovable and charming enough to get his mum to marry him. He couldn't have been bad, then. So how do you know, Maggie, that I won't be like him if I have drink in me, somewhere down the line? This is the question he always asks her, almost as if he wants to keep her aware, constantly vigilant.

He's never touched a drop of it in his whole life. As a kid he'd sit in the corner of family parties at Christmas, or just on random Fridays for no reason when his mum and dad's pals would turn up already half gone, reeking of cigarettes and carrying six-, ten-, twelve-packs of beer and bottles of cheap wine from the off-licence, and watch them. His parents' personalities would change in the space of a couple of hours. While he chomped his pickled onion Monster Munch, they'd get slowly but surely wasted and start arguments with their friends and each other over everything and nothing. About football, about politics, about television, about old films and music, about who was the best band in the world. His dad said The Rolling Stones, his mum argued Fleetwood Mac, their friends would throw their own bands in until the living room was a swirling hot soup of band names and words, and everyone would swim and thrash and some would drown in a sea of fists and feet. And Paul would just cover his ears, or escape to his room.

When the friends left his mum and dad would carry on whichever was the last argument, and their words would become more vicious and mean, until sometimes, extreme times, they'd throw things at each other. Lamps, plates, saucepans, and on one occasion the iron.

The iron was his dad's missile. Heavy and deadly, it missed his mum by a hair's breadth. He'd not been sorry.

He'd not been sorry the night he hit her across her face with the heavy frying pan and she flew across the kitchen and landed in the corner by the bin. She hadn't moved or tried to stand up, and was down there for at least three minutes while his drunken, staggering dad carried on making bacon sandwiches. It took a crying terrified Paul to call 999 and shake his mother to a consciousness that was fleeting and intermittent.

She survived; it had been more of a glancing blow than it looked and her own drunkenness and therefore precarious footing had made it seem worse than it was.

But it was bad. And things only got worse. Eventually, thankfully, his dad started hitting people outside the house, and this led to him being imprisoned and having a restraining order put on him so he couldn't contact his family. Of course, he did, several times over the years when he got out of prison, and from time to time his mum let him back in the house. It was only when he reached adulthood and moved out that Paul was really free.

Sometimes Maggie sees the ghosts from his past in his eyes. She sees those memories come calling, and they aren't friendly callers.

She knows all about the bad memories. She's an expert.

34

THEN

Memory is a powerful weapon that can be used against you at any time.

Maggie's memory is mostly of silence, but inside the silence is fear, disgust, even wonder.

At the time – the first first time, which wasn't really a time because it wasn't penetrative – she'd wondered how the churchyard had been empty for so long, long enough for it to happen. She'd wondered why no one had come out. At the second first time, which was a real first time, she'd wondered why Franny had left the tent and not come back, and how he'd managed to leave his unnoticed for so long, and how he'd not been caught in the act.

She'd felt disgust at the smell of him, the feel of his skin, the roughness of his face, the grunts that came from his hot, stinky mouth.

She'd felt fear at the pain between her legs, imagined herself tearing; fear of the blood that came and continued for a couple of days.

So many potential first times over the years she'd dismissed, refused, ran from – apart from once, in Greece, with a bottle of retsina and a chaser of blind hope. So, the third first time, which had been the second real first time, had been fumbling and fast, and of course she'd never seen Andros again.

And now... there is now.

Paul has always told her it's not his intention to scare her or pressure her, so she's always felt safe with him. He's always told her she's the boss of herself and everything she does. Whatever she chooses to do or not do, is fine with him, and if, along the way, things happen that derail her, he'll be there to help her back onto the track, but only if she wants him to.

'You're so strong, Maggie,' he tells her now. 'You don't need me. You might think you do sometimes, but I know it's not true. All I can hope, though, is that you want me. Just here I mean.'

She tells him she does want him. She wants him to be with her, to laugh with her, to chase away the bear with her.

And now, she wants him to make love to her.

The real first time is now. When she eventually accepts him, it's the first time she's ever felt real love, real intimacy. He gives it so easily and with such gentleness she doesn't feel one ounce of fear, or pain, or regret.

But the bear is lying under their bed, listening to their moans of love, and it has plans.

35

THEN

Being happy with a man is hard when you've seen your best friend brutalised, traumatised, and watched them shrink away from men. Franny holds much guilt over the fact she's feeling the butterflies with Steve. She thinks it means she's off her guard, or at least that it'll threaten to take her off it.

He's so handsome she wants to faint whenever she sees him, like one of those silly cartoon characters swooning. She won't ever let him know that, though. Men are best when they don't know how much you like them. They work harder. And swooning is so stupid. She hates fawning women.

She'll never be one. She'll never submit.

She has to be the strong one anyway, and keep her eye on Maggie. Her new guy, Paul, seems okay – has passed a lot of Franny's stringent tests.

But her priority, right now, is Steve.

After their "safety net" meeting at Odder, where they'd stayed after Maggie and Paul left for dinner, Steve took her to the cinema to see some film she'll never recall, because all she can remember is the heat from his thigh alongside hers, and the way he gently grazed her hand with his throughout.

They slept together that night, which is her usual thing, and afterwards, she kind of regretted it, because she wanted to be more to him than an easy fuck, and she definitely wanted him to be more than that to her. She wanted it to go somewhere.

To her delight it did go somewhere, and she appears to mean more to him than the quick and easy lay she feared. Now, they're as much of an item as Paul and Maggie, and as a foursome they're happy, they're sociable, and they're presenting to the world as normal.

But each couple is growing a destructive embryo inside, birth date yet unknown.

36

NOW

The eighty-fifth punch comes just after they've finished eating tea. The dishes aren't even done. Franny rubs at her jaw with no emotion. After the elation of getting the contract, the come down has left her numb. She can't even feel the pain.

She decides to leave. This number of punches is ridiculous.

It's taken approximately thirteen years of courtship and fourteen months of marriage to rack up that number of hits, and most of the blows have come in the last eight weeks. She thinks it's because of the vodka he's drinking; more and more of it every night, until his red and watery eyes can hardly see beyond his boxer's reach in front of him.

But she's always in range. Her own drinking – as much gin as she can consume without dying – doesn't make things any easier. She never seems to be able to get out of his way.

She swears she has a permanent dent in her solar plexus; a groove that fits his hand perfectly. It's like a rock that's softened and moulded with the rhythm of sea spray, or tree bark sculpted by the beak of a woodpecker looking for food. She once read that woodpeckers choose dead trees, or weak ones like birch or willow, because they're easier to carve and easier to extract insects from.

She feels weak. She feels plundered and empty. If she takes it any longer, she'll be a dead tree.

When she was a little girl, she was strong like an ash. Her mother always told her so, and in her company she always was. She remembers it plain as day. Always laughing, always being cherished, always marching through life and puddles with wellies and a fierce armour deep in her chest. An armour that had been put there with love and devotion, and a million words in torrents like a rushing river through a deep gorge; *You are amazing, you are smart, you are worthy, you are powerful, you are everything, you are treasured, you are loved loved loved.*

She was lucky to have that, especially when Maggie had had her dad taken so early, before he'd finished telling her how fabulous she was.

She thought her right to all that went when she left home, but it didn't... it didn't. She's starting to see that now. She's not waiting around for punch number eighty-six.

She is everything, she is amazing, she *will* be loved.

It's just a matter of when and how. Earlier, she almost told Maggie. She was so close, but then the phone call had come about her grandfather, so the moment had been lost.

Tomorrow, she'll take herself somewhere and think.

37

NOW

Her granddad always loved science. He'd once told her there's about twenty watts of power in the average body – enough to power a light bulb. Maggie peers down at him now, all shrunken and sunken on the pillow, and slight as a kitten under his crocheted blanket. There's a forty-watt bulb shining on him from the bedside table, and she thinks that makes four people in the room: him, her and the lamp. It makes her feel less lonely, less empty.

When her gran comes in with soup, she tells her to put it on the side and that she'll make sure he eats.

'I won't make you, Granddad,' she whispers, looking into his eyes. 'Gran's soup, eh?'

It won't be eaten. He's too far gone. Her gran has only made it for something to do.

She remembers his legendary appetite – even for his wife's soup – and the way he was always full of vigour, of mischief. Her eyes land on the photo of her and him that's under the lamp. He's so big in it. So present. Playing football in the backyard; she remembers the day well. He'd been lean, muscly, a ball of kinetic energy. Even though he was a way older grandfather than most of her friends', he was scrappy and strong. She loved that about him, along with all the other things she loved; far too many to count. Since her dad died, he'd been her number one. Always there, always present not only in body but in mind and heart. He always had loads of time for her, made her his priority. It was no exaggeration to say he'd saved her life so many times, just by being there. She can't imagine him *not* being in her life. Can't imagine he'll ever truly be gone.

He once told her energy can't be created or destroyed. That it had always been there since the Big Bang, and it always would.

'It's just moved around, repurposed,' he'd said, and he'd put a small mound of dirt in her hand and told her to close her eyes and imagine the millions of people whose particles were probably in there; trillions of atoms that had been blown around since time began. She'd found it strangely comforting, had asked 'Is daddy in there?' and had been overjoyed when he'd said 'Yes, he's there. He always will be'.

'Photons are bouncing around all the time,' he'd said. 'They're landing on you. They're disturbed by your smile, and they gather in your eyes.'

His eyes are dimmer now.

She asks him if he'll take some water. He smiles and she sees photons ready to leave his mouth, so she leans in and catches them in a kiss on her cheek. As she holds a sponge to his lips, in his eyes are particles of love she knows have already been repurposed in the chambers of her heart.

Just after midnight there's a shift in the atmosphere of the room. Maggie and her gran are sitting, slumped, in chairs either side of the bed. Her granddad has made a noise and it's shaken them both from their semi-sleep.

'Gramps,' Maggie says softly and she moves her chair closer, takes his hand which is resting on the blanket. There are dark purple bruises on the back of it that weren't there earlier. She rubs them with her thumb. Something inside her chest is hardening and her throat starts to close. It's near now. This bruising is one of the signs.

Her granddad starts to mumble so she moves closer. He hasn't spoken for a couple of weeks and has just lain quietly, his big eyes sometimes taking things in and sometimes not. Mostly not.

'Hey, Gramps, Gran and I are both here. It's a lovely afternoon. You should see the sunshine.'

The room is filled with rays of sunlight, and in them a million dust particles float, taking their part in the dance of jumbled mutterings from Maggie's granddad's mouth. The sounds he makes are more notes than words, and Maggie and her grandmother sit, silent aural witnesses to the symphony. Maggie imagines she understands what he's saying, and in her heart she truly does. He's singing about a life well-lived, a family well-loved, and a world well and truly travelled.

He's ninety-nine years old and there are no regrets from anyone in this room. He lived a life that meant something, and he's had the most love anyone could have. Now it's time for him to leave and scatter his particles elsewhere.

Maggie's grandmother takes his other hand. She leans in to kiss his cheek and says: 'Go gently, dear Harold. You mattered. I love you and will *always* love you.'

He takes his final breath shortly after 6pm. Maggie watches as her grandmother straightens the crocheted blanket on his bed, and the dust particles containing him and her father waltz together in the light of the sun.

38

NOW

On the way home, Maggie remembers her mum can't get ITV. In the grand scheme of things – at least in a normal person's life – this is small fry, but to her mum, it's huge, and Maggie reckons she will have to push her grief down for now and go and sort her out.

The ITV debacle is even huger to her mum than learning her father-in-law is dead, it appears, because when Maggie tells her, she shrugs and says, 'He was really old, Margaret. If you want a brew, put the kettle on.'

Maggie is shocked by this, even though her mum is always pretty blunt these days and hasn't seen her granddad for several years. She kept in touch with him when Maggie was younger, because of course they visited fairly often, but when Maggie grew up and started visiting her granddad on her own, her mum stepped back.

Maggie's mum is seventy but looks a lot older. She's not looked after herself. She wallows in the past, and this is why Maggie hates coming home.

'I'm sick of absolutely everything,' she says as Maggie brings a mug of tea over. Before she takes the tea, she guzzles the dregs of a glass of gin. Maggie tries to mentally count how much money she has in her purse right now. Card readers are not working and her mum might ask for another bottle. The scene is never pretty when her mum runs out.

'Get me another,' her mother says. She swipes the back of her hand across her mouth, pulling her red lipstick into a lopsided Joker smile. Maggie wants to smooth it away with her thumb, or with a handkerchief with spit, like her mum used to do for her back when she wasn't sick of absolutely everything.

'Okay, later,' she says, and takes the glass from her hand; replaces it with the mug of tea. She needs a different liquid inside her.

She's been drinking gin ever since Maggie's dad died, and that's a long and drunken twenty-nine years. She doesn't drink it because she likes it, she's very fond of telling Maggie. She drinks it because it keeps everything down; the despair she feels. Everyone's gone, she says. Everyone that meant anything. Her dad, her mum, her best friend, the love of her life.

He was also the love of mine, Maggie wants to say.

'Why are they all leaving?' she asks again, because she asks this every time. Maggie tells her that's how it works. Her mum cries so hard she turns herself inside out, and Maggie closes her eyes against the sight of her raw flesh.

She tells Maggie she's going, bit by bit. That whenever she looks in the mirror another part of her has fallen off and she can't find it. 'Have you looked in the Dyson,' Maggie jokes, but she sees it; she's fading.

She tells Maggie the pain is getting worse. Her bones are crumbling. Her body is eating itself. Most days when Maggie visits, she's on the sofa where she left her, and the putrid puddle of her stares up at Maggie, silently asking questions she can't answer.

'I'm sick of absolutely everything,' she says again, so Maggie goes to sit beside her and lets her lie against her bosom like she once lay against hers. She wants her not to be sick anymore, not to be alone. She wants her to know she's there.

Maggie ignores that her mum's cheekbones are knives; that the body in her arms is made of sharp coat hangers. She just holds her, because everyone she loves is leaving one after the other and she wants to hold on to this woman, despite everything.

'I'll get ITV back for you, Mum,' she promises. 'Let's just rest for a while.'

She feels as exhausted as her mum must be. Without her dad, neither of them has much inside them anymore.

39

THEN

'Your dad isn't feeling so well today, love,' Cynthia says. She's in the kitchen making breakfast when Maggie comes down. Maggie sees the blue striped eggcups on their blue striped plates – just the two places laid today.

Boiled egg and soldiers is Maggie's favourite breakfast. She and her dad always race to see who can finish the yolk first, dipping the golden-brown toast in bite after bite until all the yellow has gone. Then, when her dad goes upstairs to shave, her mum always brings the yolk back – a trick she's been doing for Maggie since she was two.

'There,' she says, after dropping a knife-edge of butter into the eggshell lined with white. 'Abracadabra, wait for the magic, Maggie.'

And Maggie's eyes would widen as the yolk seemed to materialise again before her eyes. And even when she eventually figured it out, she never let on to her mum because she knew she liked making magic for her.

But today, there's no competition so she eats her egg slowly, not really tasting it. Her dad's not played eating games with her for a couple of weeks.

'Will Daddy be coming down in time for dinner?' she asks. Her mum takes a hanky out of her apron pocket and blows her nose into it. Her hands are shaking, and her nails are bitten down. This is unusual for her mother, who is always so nicely turned out.

'He'll try, love, but I'm not sure. Shall we do something together? Just you and me?'

They go to the park, and Maggie runs around with the other children who are there, leaving her mother sitting on a bench. Whenever Maggie looks round to see how she is, she finds her in exactly the same position. She has her hands joined together and slotted between her thighs, like she's keeping them warm, but it's a lovely sunny day and not cold at all. When she sees Maggie looking, she smiles with only her mouth.

They stay in the park until it's time to go back for dinner.

Her father doesn't come down.

40

NOW

It's hard not to be able to share the news about her granddad on her social media. That would be the easier option. Despite its obvious down sides, being able to tweet or just post something on Facebook, knowing it'll get around to everyone at the same time, is so much easier than picking up the landline and ringing everyone in her own and her grandmother's address book. The cumbersome address book her granddad had said she'd need one day.

You're right, Gramps. Today is the day I need this old-fashioned thing we call paper and ink.

Being a Catholic and a massive noise in the parish and community, Harold's funeral is set for this Saturday, so time is of the essence. By the end of the morning, Maggie is drained, physically and emotionally.

Her emotions are so mixed up. No one was surprised that a ninety-nine-year-old man died, but he was a precious husband, father and grandfather for so many years and his loss is such a wrench. It makes her think of her father too, which is always a dangerous thing. She's tried for so long to keep that suppressed.

That loss in itself is so painful because her dad wasn't there when she was going through the most difficult time of her life.

By 11am, she's done, but finds she can't face work, so calls Franny and says she's taking the morning off. On a whim, she calls her therapist and luckily he has a slot if she can make it within the hour.

'My granddad died,' she says bluntly as she walks through the door of his office.

'Shit,' he says, which makes Maggie laugh out loud, but also causes something in her heart to lock up like a fist is squeezing it. It is indeed shit. 'I'm so sorry. Do you want to talk about that?'

'Not really. I mean, it's fine. He was old and you can't keep them forever, right? My heart is heavy but... it's triggered me. Losing people... It's getting to be a fucking awful pattern in my life. I either lose them, have them ripped from me, or throw them away.'

Maggie sits on the couch and finds a spot to focus on behind Taylor Clarke's head.

'I think I want... to talk about all the things in the box.'

41

THEN

Wasdale Head is like paradise, if paradise is hordes of screaming kids, frantic booze-craving teachers, and skies so clear and blue it's like looking into the eyes of God. Maggie knows it might not stay that way – that it could get cloudy, stormy, dangerous – but right now it looks like a painting on a chocolate box, and she feels peace for the first time in a long time.

She tilts her head back and looks up at Scafell Pike. It makes her dizzy. Her dad once told her the surest way to get to Heaven is to make the effort and climb a mountain. Up there, he said, the air is clean and all the sounds from Earth are muted and muffled. Then, it's easier to ask questions because you have the space in your mind to find them. And it's also easier to hear the answers, when there are no other voices to distract you from what God is saying.

She's a little bit angry with God though, despite her good mood today. Well, a lot angry, because he let her dad die, even though he'd climbed three mountains and always went to church. Maggie wonders if he ever asked whether the cancer would disappear. Maybe he had asked that, and maybe the answer had been no.

'Margaret Milburn, come and prepare your tent,' Mr Roberts calls from the throng of kids and teachers. Maggie considers pretending she hasn't heard, so she can keep this cloak of peacefulness and wonder at the beauty of the mountain for a while longer; considers telling him the howling of the wind is too noisy, but she knows he won't let up.

He's given her a hard time ever since the incident in his classroom. She'd stayed behind to clear the desks because it had been her turn, and she'd dropped all the pencils and they'd skittered all over, causing him to tut loudly and give her a look she didn't like. She'd dropped to her knees to scoop them up and he'd said: 'Are you this stupid at home, Margaret Milburn?' For a second she'd felt his hand, heavy on the back of her neck, and it had lingered there a few beats too long until she felt a sweat forming on her forehead and on her chest, and all she'd wanted to do was stand and run from the room as fast as she could.

But he said she had to pick every pencil up, and when she had them all in her hands, she raised her head and he was there, inches away. She saw his legs and his clenched hands and could hear his breath; sounding like her breath did when she played netball or did cross-country. Short and panting and strained. There had been a moment of silence so loud she'd heard it ringing in her ears, and as he'd flinched to move even closer to her, the classroom door had opened and he'd spun away like a starting gun had been fired. Maggie had never felt so relieved as she did then to see the Head standing there and clearing her throat, saying to Mr Roberts she'd like to talk to him. Maggie was relieved though she didn't know why. He'd always been such an inspiring teacher. All the children liked him.

He calls again for Maggie to come and sort out her tent, and this pulls her back to the present. She drags her eyes away from the green, yellow and brown of the mountain against the aching blue of the sky, and towards the multicoloured canvases blotted around with kids lolloping in their crunchy kagools and rubber wellies, giggling and shouting and erupting with excitement like volcanoes. This is all too much, Maggie thinks. Way, way too much. She's at the place her dad told her she could speak to God, and that should be good but all she has is memories – of her dad, of her own stupidity, and she... Just. Wants. To. Be. Quiet.

As she unrolls her sleeping bag, she hears the zip and a shadow falls over her as she kneels on the groundsheet. The air inside the tent is suddenly warmer; diffused light falling through the canvas and projecting the sleeping bag shadow into the corner. She knows he's behind her and she holds her breath.

'This is a very cosy tent, Margaret,' Mr Roberts says. He's standing outside with his head thrust in. His usually tidy beard is unruly, like he hasn't bothered with any grooming for a few days. He looks like a wild animal.

'Yes, it is,' Maggie says. 'It's for me and Frances.' Not for you, she wants to add.

'I'm sure you'll be very comfy in here,' he says, and moves further in. His hand reaches down to feel the sleeping bag. 'Oh yes, soft.'

He pulls his hand away from the bag and just before he leaves, it touches Maggie's leg, just above her knee, and lingers there for a double beat.

42

NOW

'I know all this is hard for you, Maggie,' Taylor Clarke says. His pen is a blur on the surface of his pad. Maggie is always amazed at how he can talk and write at the same time. 'But it's really important you push the door open now it's ajar.'

'When is a door not a door?' Maggie suddenly says, then, 'Don't know where that came from. Probably one of my dad's jokes.'

'Just relax. Take your time.'

Funny how Maggie has never noticed before how gentle and kind Taylor Clarke's eyes are. He looks nothing like a rapist, and she's suddenly sorry for ever giving him that nickname. He actually looks a bit like her dad, just in his demeanour, and around his eyes, which have lines she thinks must come from smiling a lot. From *feeling*.

'What's the first thing in the box, Maggie?' He sits with his pen poised.

'I guess since I already told you about the St Christopher, when talking about my dad, I'll tell you about the charcoal rubbing.'

'Then let's start there. Let's push this door open.'

43

THEN

Maggie and Frances are in the graveyard, giggling. Everyone else is inside the church, but they've escaped because they can't trust themselves not to laugh while Mr Roberts and Miss Harper tell the story of St Olaf, and how the church is the smallest parish church in England and the brick structure has stood here since 1525, although it would've been made of wood before that and is probably all in all a thousand years old.

The reason this information makes Maggie and Frances giggle is because it's a rumour amongst the school kids that Miss Harper is about a thousand years old. She has grey hair and a fine beard of whiskers curling from her chin, and according to legend she's looked exactly the same ever since the school opened seventy years ago. David Arnold says his dad, and his dad's dad, and his dad's dad's dad, remember her always being there. Everyone believes she has a picture in the attic like Dorian Gray, only there's a fault and the picture looks young and pretty and she's an old wrinkled crone.

'Do you think her and Mr Roberts are at it?' Frances asks. She's plonked herself down next to one of the old gravestones and has tucked her skirt between her outstretched legs.

'Ew, no, I don't think so!' Maggie is horrified at the thought of them being 'at it'; at the thought of Mr Roberts at it, particularly. She doesn't want to think of him sweaty and grunting. 'Did you have to put that thought into my head.'

Frances laughs. 'He has a thing for you, Mags.'

'Don't. Seriously. Anyway, I need to do my gravestone rubbing.' Maggie consults the list of tasks they had all been given at the start of the day. She wants to ignore what Frances has just said because she's afraid she could be right.

Frances is bored with checking things off her list, and leaves Maggie to her rubbing to go inside where the rest of the group is. Maggie imagines how cramped and stuffy it must be with twenty-five kids and two adults, all packed into that one small room. With him.

Outside in the graveyard, Maggie tries to show respect for the graves on which she's standing, tiptoeing carefully round where she thinks the people are lying underneath, although it's hard to tell on some of them. She thinks the headstones look sad, worn smooth mostly with green moss showing their neglect. It's quite dark because the sun is hiding behind the trees, shadows through their leaves and branches painting arms and fingers onto the grass and the stones, so it looks like the people beneath are trying to get out. Apparently, some people who fell while climbing the mountains nearby are buried here. Maggie wonders what it would've felt like if her dad had died climbing a mountain instead of after a battle with cancer. She's not sure which death is more terrible or painful. Probably about the same, but one would be quicker.

She needs to work quickly and then get back to the others, because being here amongst death is giving her the creeps, and she doesn't want to think of her dad. She thinks it's disrespectful to make a rubbing of someone's epitaph, because each of these people was loved like she loved him, and they're missed like she misses him.

With the paper in one hand and her charcoal stick in the other, she works quickly on a stone she can just about read. It's a woman, aged thirty-five, who died in a year she can't quite make out. But it's a long time ago. People died so young in the olden days. They had so many illnesses doctors didn't understand or know how to treat. But then, not much has changed, or her dad would still be here.

She feels him before she hears him. A warmth, behind her thigh, then a pressure against it and her bottom. A hot breath of air on her neck that blows the stray hairs of her ponytail away from her skin. Then his voice, unmistakable.

'Margaret Milburn. Always the rebel. Always off on your own. How's the rubbing going?' She'd not heard him approach. Her stomach churns at the suddenness of him.

She can't speak or move. He moves closer, until her body is pressed against the headstone. It's one of those crosses with a circle at the top; she grabs it to steady herself, dropping her charcoal onto the grass as she does so. Her head is close to the cross and she's looking out of the top cut-out bit at the centre, so she sees the rest of the churchyard in four different segments of green and brown. The church door in the top right one. Will it open? Will anyone see? Will this stop?

He's doing that breathing noise, but louder. Presses harder against the top of her thighs. Moving in a slow rhythmic motion which starts to get faster. Maggie's face is pushed firmly against the cross and now the four segments of her vision are blurry. She feels moisture on her face, but she feels nothing else. Nothing inside.

But outside she feels the pressure, the pressure, and hears his breathing faster and faster until at last it stops, the movement and the breath. And he moves back, causing Maggie to fall to her knees in front of the gravestone, where the name of the dead young woman is right in front of her. Her name is Margaret too.

Maggie doesn't look round. Doesn't dare to move. But she sees him, walking slowly into the church without a backward glance, and when he walks through the door, she hears him.

'Children, settle down. Settle down. Don't make me tell you again.'

And Maggie fears this isn't over. They have one more night and one more day here. Mr Roberts is circling her as an eagle would circle a rabbit, from a height way too distant to be able to do anything. She's in the path of his swoop. And she can't escape it.

44

NOW

Since Maggie isn't going to be in, Franny decides to take the morning off too; Kelly is more than capable of running things by herself for a morning. Steve seems in a strangely convivial mood, which makes her suspicious of what's to come, but she decides to go with it. He wants them to go somewhere for the morning; she'd have preferred to be by herself, to think, but she reckons she'll be able to ditch him for a while at some point.

He takes her to Sealife at the Trafford Centre because he has some free tickets he won in a raffle at work. It's strange to walk around here with him like they're a normal couple doing a normal thing. There's a party of school kids running around in their uniforms, screeching and shouting. It's actually a welcome excuse not to talk to Steve, the loudness. Franny finds herself wondering what her life would be like if they'd had kids. Steve had lost interest in the idea quite early on when she wasn't barefoot and pregnant right away, as had been his wish. He could be stubborn and childish that way.

He'd had a vasectomy without even consulting her.

Now, she thanks her lucky stars they'd never brought children into their marriage. But maybe it's not too late for her.

She's young and relatively healthy – if she ditches the drinking. And now the gambling apps and websites aren't working, she can start healing from that too.

She stops in front of a tank of octopuses and watches their elegant dancing. It's like they have inner peace because they know something beautiful, some secret to happiness.

She wishes they could share it. What she needs now more than anything is to know there's something lovely out there, in her future. She needs to know there's hope.

45

NOW

Octopus. Class: Cephalopoda. Subclass: Coleoidea. Legends portray it as dangerous, but it displays intelligence, ingenuity, and often fierce love.

Man. Order: Primate. Species: Homo Sapiens. With abundant texts and studies, characteristics include compassion, love, and the capability to reason and environmentally adapt, but also to commit acts of extreme violence and cruelty.

Light shines through the glass like a diamond shard.

The ring – as he put it on her finger – had felt cool. Felt right. She'd been a sunburst of happiness.

Behind the thick glass, rocks and coral formations shelter creatures of all shapes and sizes; each uniquely beautiful.

He loved her for her, he'd said. But he'd tried to remould her from the start. Tried to change her hues; the very essence of her. The prisms of her inner colours morphed into his.

From behind the largest rock, Franny catches sight of a tentacle, then another, and another, twisting through the water like a dance of eight veils; a body undulating like the world is watching but it doesn't care.

On their wedding day they'd danced in front of guests they could barely see. Life – their world – was just them, his arms around her strong and loving and safe.

The octopus flutters around and attaches itself to the glass in front of her face. Its suckers are fixed fast and unmoving, but she sees the flesh of the octopus tremble in tiny breaths and pulses. If the glass wasn't there, it would be on her face. Smothering and taking her air.

Years after their first dance she's started to breathe in short gasps because her air is scarce. The arms that held her in love have morphed and multiplied until they obstruct, stifle. She can no longer remember the first anger, the first shouting, the first blow. Only knows she needs it to stop. She needs it to come to an end.

She watches the creature loosen its hold on the glass; wonders if it's that easy.

46

NOW

It seems like it's taken three hours to get the churchyard story out, but it's only been about fifty minutes. Maggie needs something, preferably alcohol, but she settles for coffee.

'Do you want one?' she asks as she puts a pod in and places a cup underneath.

'I'm fine, thanks,' Taylor replies. He's deep into writing something in his pad, and his face is ruffled. Maggie feels marginally guilty that she's responsible for replacing his kind and gentle eyes with dark and troubled ones.

'How happy are you to continue, Maggie?' he asks as she takes her seat again.

'Mmm... on a scale of one to ten, about a minus fifty?' Maggie suggests, taking a sip of coffee. It's not wine, but it'll do. It'll eventually hit her jangling nerves and stretch them into another, more manageable, shape.

'Well, since the hour is almost up, bar about ten minutes, why don't we move away from it a little? Take a breather?'

'I'd like that. I need it.' Maggie says. She feels like she's been through the mangle on an old twin tub washing machine. Every part of her is pulled thin and flat.

'When is your grandfather's funeral? Is that okay, to talk about?'

'Sure.' Maggie smiles. 'It's this Saturday. It's quick, but he was like the don of our parish. Gran made a joke, which shocked me, but at least she's kept her humour. She said, he's so old, they daren't leave it any longer, as he's half decomposed anyway.'

Taylor laughs politely, and then looks at his watch. Maggie knows it's his way of saying: I have another appointment, and you must leave. She never takes offence at that. The man is busy.

'Can I see you tomorrow?' Maggie asks. 'I know I'm needy right now, but with the funeral and everything, I just want to get myself straight, you know?'

'Of course. Just a second.' He gets up and fetches the diary from his desk, flips through it. 'Good job I always keep written records of everything and don't rely on technology. I'd be screwed.'

'Yeah,' Maggie says. 'What the heck is happening in the world?'

'Beats me.' He scratches his head. 'Pulses from outer space people are saying.'

'Sounds very "Close Encounters" to me,' Maggie says. 'But somehow, I prefer to think of that than any alternative. State of the world these days, you never know who is messing with what.'

'Indeed. Okay, yes, I've an opening tomorrow at noon. How's that?'

'I'll make it work, thank you.'

'My pleasure, Maggie. Will you be okay until then?'

Maggie drains the rest of her coffee before she answers. She has a particular job to do that she isn't looking forward to.

'I'll be fine, just as soon as I tell a very dear friend that one of his most favourite people in the world has died.'

47

NOW

It's not easy. Even before she picks up the phone, Maggie is sweating. She doesn't want to think of Paul sad, and she doesn't want to be the one who upsets him. But she knows it has to be her because she doesn't want him to hear it somewhere else.

When Paul answers the phone, Maggie hears a commotion in the background. It sounds like his home is under siege, or a herd of elephants has stormed it. She forgot he has the boys this week.

'Hello. George! Put that back and stop annoying your brother! Sorry, hello.'

'Jesus, if I'd known you were hosting a mixed martial arts event, I'd have chosen another day.' Maggie can't help but laugh.

'Mags. Shit. Sorry about that. It's like world war fucking three in here. Let me just shut the door. Aaron, let him play with it. Jeez, can you just give me a minute of peace?'

The sound becomes muffled as Paul apparently moves away from the terror, into another room.

'Sorry, Mags. This is all my fault. I let them have birthday cake before *and* after tea. 'Sup?'

'My gramps died, Paul.'

'Oh fuck, Mags. No,' Paul says and then goes silent for a minute or two. Maggie doesn't feel the need to ask if he's still there. She can hear him breathing; it's fast, like he's struggling.

She closes her eyes and remembers the sound of his breathing when he slept. Sometimes he'd roll over and his hot breath would be on her face. When they made love and he held her after, she'd feel his breath in her hair.

She misses his breathing.

'It sucks. I wanted to tell you the funeral is on Saturday, and of course you'll come, right?'

'No question. Of course.' His voice is flat.

'Okay, I'll see you on Thursday, for our drink, and give you all the details. Text me to let me know where to meet you. Oh, shit! You can't. Fucking mobiles! Hang on, I'll get a pen.'

As Maggie fetches a pen and pad, she's suddenly overwhelmed. Her gramps, who saved her life many times, is dead. Paul would've been there for her, had they still been together.

But she fucked that up royally.

48

THEN

The mirror needs a wipe, so Franny fetches a bit of kitchen roll and gives it a polish. She's faffing around in Maggie's old bedroom at her mum's house, waiting for Maggie to finish in her mum's room. They've decided it's the best place to get ready because Paul's been staying at Maggie's flat and they need to be apart the night before. She can hardly wait for her to put her dress on and come out and do the big reveal. Franny knows what the dress looks like, but she can't wait to see it on. She's beside herself with excitement.

What greets her, though, when the door finally opens, is Maggie dressed in jeans and her Smiths T-shirt, hair in a ponytail, mascara all down her cheeks.

'What the fuck, Mags! It's almost eleven. Why aren't you dressed?'

'I can't do it, Franny.' Maggie's eyes are wide and her pupils look like black poker chips. The last time Franny saw a living thing this frightened, it had been her old cat, Munchkin, when the family Staffordshire bull terrier had cornered it in the conservatory one Christmas.

'What do you mean, you can't...'

'I just can't. I've made a mistake. Do you think I've made a mistake, Fran?'

'It's a bit late in the fucking day to start thinking that.' Franny puts her hand in her hair, pulls at it in disbelief. Downstairs she can hear Maggie's mum opening the door, so she looks out of the window. It's the florist.

'The fucking flowers are here, Mags! And, and, and back at your flat, right this second, the best fucking man you'll *ever* meet, is putting his suit and tie on, and sticking a fucking carnation in his lapel, and his best man is patting his pocket to check he has the rings before they head to the church.'

'I know, I know. Stop crowding my head.' Maggie sits down on the bed. She feels desperate. She feels like she's falling. Paul doesn't deserve this.

But didn't he say to her, right at the beginning, when she'd told him about what had happened, at Scafell Pike and later, that he'd understand if she wanted to take it slow, and at any point she wanted out, he'd understand and he wouldn't stop her.

Didn't he say that? She doesn't think he meant this late in the day, but he did say it. He did.

The last time he'd said it they'd been lying in bed, late on a Sunday morning, at the flat. The weather wasn't good, but the bedroom always caught the sun all day, and this day it had thrown a blanket of yellow warmth onto their bed. Paul usually jumped out of bed every day and made them coffee and toast – a throwback, he said, to having to be the man of the house at home, or rather, the only adult full stop as his parents waged war on each other at every opportunity and spent most of their time either pissed, on their way to being pissed, or on their way back via a battlefield full of land mines. But this morning, he'd pulled her into a warm spoon and traced his fingers delicately along the blonde hairs on her arm, which were lit by the sunshine.

'Days like this, Mags, I always find it hard to think of what happened to you. You know, back then. All of it.'

'You do believe me though, don't you?'

'What're you talking about, of course I believe you.' They'd stayed there the whole day, making love, drinking tea, making love some more. She'd felt then that all she wanted, all she needed, was there, in the bed, in the flat, in her life. She'd told him everything – about the day at the churchyard, later in the tent. About what came after. And he'd stayed. He'd stayed. She didn't think she could be any happier.

'If ever this gets too much, Maggie, I want you to promise me – promise me with your hand on your heart – to tell me, so we can fix it. Together.'

He'd pushed her hair away from her face, looked deep into her eyes. He knew the demons that lived there; knew they often came back. Knew about the bear and how it lingered, and paced, and slept sometimes but always woke up.

He'd told her he was a match for it.

She'd believed him. And when he asked her to marry him, she thought she'd never again feel as complete or as loved, or as safe.

But today, she doesn't feel safe. Today, there's a registrar and fifteen family and friends at the town hall, and a cake at The Cage, and she knows Franny has decorated their bedroom back at the flat with confetti and streamers. She's not supposed to know but she heard her on the phone with her mum. All she can think of is the bear napping in her wardrobe, waiting until she gets into bed with her new husband. And then he'll leap out, with his horrible teeth bared and Paul will see this is all real and raw instead of just something she told him, and there's no way

Maggie is ever going to be good enough or healthy enough or free enough for him to live with.

'I just can't do it, Fran,' she says. 'Please help me.'

She's breaking the promise she made with her hand on her heart, because she never told him, never talked to him so they could fix it.

And now it's too late.

49

NOW

A fierce wind is blowing outside the house, and it's making music on the wrought-iron gate at the end of the front path. It sounds like a choir of ghosts, or a pack of howling wolves, or a company of angels. It's hard to tell because the timbre changes every moment, weaving this way and that in a seductive dance of sound. Whichever it is, it isn't unpleasant, so Maggie cranks open the living-room window a bit to hear it better.

When she was forced to go to church as a child, the only thing she'd liked about it was the singing, the hymns. Even with the voices of a hundred or so reluctant kids, hymns always sounded beautiful, because the words were written and the music composed to be divine, and that was kind of hard to mess up.

She'd so wanted to believe in God when she was little, because her dad did and she saw his belief made him happy, and it certainly made him good. But she learned, as she grew older, that happiness and goodness didn't go hand in hand with believing in God. That sometimes it was definitely at odds, and despite all his faith and all his goodness, her dad got ill anyway, and died anyway, and her life was blown apart anyway... and anyway... and anyway...

Nothing ever stays good. She knows that now, aged thirty-six, with thirty years' distance from the last time she saw the man she worshipped, and twenty-four years' distance from the bad thing that happened. Had there been any such thing as God, none of it would've happened, especially not where it did: outside a place where God supposedly lived. If he existed, he'd have allowed her to stay an innocent child, unspoilt and happy, and she'd have grown up in her own time and enjoyed music like all the other girls her age, who were into East 17 and Take That. She'd have experimented with make-up and gone to Chelsea Girl and Top Shop and worn stonewash and combat boots, with her fringe all hiked up with a can of Wella, like all the pretty girls who were popular in her class.

But instead, she became the freak, the outsider, the pariah. And with her dad gone and her mother suddenly as low as any person could get, she felt terribly, utterly alone.

Still does.

Wanting to see her dad and granddad so badly, she picks up her phone. She has tons of photos on it, snapped at her mum's house one night in a bid to get them all on her SIM card. She'd sneaked up to her mum's bedroom, waded through all the cardboard boxes and piles of newspapers, and found the box where she knew it would be – in the top drawer. There were dozens and dozens of photos, maybe even a couple of hundred. She snapped every one.

Now though, she can't get the folder open. She has to click on it about ten times. When it does open, it's empty.

A coldness washes over her. She tries again. Nothing. Every photo she had on her phone, of her dad, of her gramps. None of them are there.

50

NOW

She can't avoid the truth now. They've all gone. Every one of them. Her phone is blank, has been for days, and all the news programmes point to the same thing.

Everyone has lost everything.

Everything.

It can't just be her. It's been on the news and she's tried hard to ignore it, but now it's impossible to deny.

When she finally realises there's nothing left on the hard drive, something shifts inside her, like someone is moving a heavy and bulky object, like a piano, and has dropped it on one side, causing a thud. She puts a hand to her chest and feels the lurching beat of a terrified heart. Who'll be here for her now, in the darkness of night and when she wakes up with the bear in the morning? Knowing she had someone – her gramps – was the one thing that made it all bearable. Now, she feels fear like a cancer inside her.

To Maggie, fear is stillness. She doesn't shake, or moan, or scream, or any of the things they do in films. Fear takes her mobility, takes her voice, like when she sees the bear, staring at her with his insane eyes from the bottom of the bed. Then she lies, stock-still, hardly breathing, clutching her duvet in locked fists. And now, the stillness creeps up at the thought of losing all those precious photos, all those memories she's terrified will fade.

'Oh, Dad, Gramps...' Tears run down her cheeks and there's a tightness in her chest. A swelling starts to grow, and it's made of love and sadness and total helplessness. It's rising up and she fears what it'll bring when it comes. She takes several deep breaths.

In the memory bank of her mind, she thumbs through her favourite photos. Her dad was always young in them. Because, of course, he never got old. He reached the age of thirty-six and then his body decided that was it. That was enough time walking around on Earth, enough time laughing and loving and breathing in air. It was time to go.

Only, no one was really prepared, because it happened too fast.

Most of the photos of him are black-and-white, or that strange yellow colour that screams the seventies; perfect square Polaroids whose corners are peeling back but which she flattened in cyberspace forever with her iPhone. The one that's failed her now. The colour ones are fewer, because when he started to feel ill, he didn't like his photo being taken. She hadn't realised that at the time, of course, but understands it now.

She screws up her eyes. There's a colour one of him and Gramps at Blackpool, with the tower behind to their right. Her dad is grinning in that way he always did when he was about to get up to mischief and do one of his silly pranks. Her granddad looked huge. It was their last time together as a family at Blackpool. The last time her dad had really laughed from his belly without bringing up a gut full of pain.

She makes a note to ask her mother for the photos. She must still have them in the box in her bedroom. Upstairs with all the crap she let accumulate before she gave up trying to get to her bed and started sleeping downstairs on the sofa.

But that will mean speaking to her, and twice in one week is too much. Maggie goes to bed with her head full of so much; memories coming in tidal waves to her dreams.

51

NOW

Memories of her dad burn like a dry log. There was a singer whose music he used to play all the time because *his* dad liked him. The singer had a deep, gravelly voice and sang about a burning ring of fire. Sometimes she'd catch her dad singing along and it was like the voice from his lips melded with the voice from the CD like some magical trick.

Whenever they went on family day trips, mostly to Blackpool, he'd sing it in the car – the light-blue Ford Cortina they'd named Genevieve, which was probably too grand a name for a car that was always breaking down and leaving them on the hard shoulder.

Genevieve had hot leather upholstery and ashtrays that smelled of nicotine and orange peel, and sometimes the smoke fug from the front seats was so thick she could almost chew it. Her dad gave up smoking after the diagnosis, but it was too little too late. He was only around for another year so he might as well have carried on.

Now, she has a recurring dream in which she chases him through a huge house with many rooms. He's always in the next room, then the next, and she never quite reaches him. But in every room is a huge black crow, perched on cushions, or tables, or large untidy stacks of DVDs with titles like *Father Dear Father*, *Father of the Bride* or *The Lost Father*, and she wakes up with tears on her face. It's such a textbook dream, but disturbing as hell.

Some days she lies in bed for a long time after waking, playing 'Ring of Fire' on a loop in her head, and wonders what happened to Genevieve.

Her dad's eyes were the same colour as Genevieve. The old cliché would have her describe them as deep pools, or an ocean, but she remembers them as so much more than that. When he was happy and laughing, they were the blue of a field of bluebells, nodding and dancing in a spring breeze. When he was sad, and when he was ill, they were the blue of a storm building up and moving in, and when it broke it filled his eyes with rain and pain.

Sadly, what she remembers most is the storm colour, and the rain. Often he cried because his insides hurt so much. Maggie sometimes tries to imagine how it feels to have your vital organs rotting inside you, and to be strangled and smothered by rapidly growing cells that are being zapped with chemicals that make you vomit and lose even the good parts of yourself.

Her dad always tried to be brave, for her. He called her a brave warrior so often through her life, and he didn't want her to see his fear at the end.

But she did see it. And she realised the thing about fear is... there's no shame in it. People often try to be brave because they think it's weak to be fearful. But Maggie thinks the opposite. She thinks feeling fear and carrying on anyway is one of the bravest things in the world. Her dad looked directly into the face of fear and stared it down, remained positive, carried on giving his love and advice, and never once felt sorry for himself or expected others to do so.

And her granddad – he was the real hero. She can't believe her two amazing role models have gone.

52

NOW

Dorothy is making her husband's bed for the last time. She wants it to look nice even though he's no longer in it. First, she removes the crocheted blanket and sets it aside to give to Maggie later.

Bending down to tuck the sheet into a hospital corner, something catches her eye under the bed. It's a faded pale-blue box that's vaguely familiar.

She reaches for the box and pulls it out. It's made from what looks like painted planks roughly joined with brass hinges. The paint is peeling off so the dull brown shows between the jagged clouds of blue. And she remembers; Harold painted this when their son, Charles, was born and said he'd one day show him what was inside. But he never did, because no matter how he tried he could never bring himself to talk about those days. And he wouldn't let anyone else.

The planks were from a hut he'd slept many nights in during the war. He had told Dorothy they reminded him of the good men he'd shared a roof with. The hut had been destroyed by bombing, and he'd salvaged the wood and made the box before coming home. He'd used it for his paltry belongings and the letters he'd managed to keep, and painted it when they'd been expecting. Dorothy knew what was inside. Along with the letters and keepsakes were medals won for honour and valour, and for helping save the lives of many of his friends. She was proud of him, but she knew he didn't wear his pride the same way; didn't consider himself brave.

She takes the medals out and lays them gently on the bed, smoothing down the scarlet and blue ribbons. She takes out the letters from friends and sweethearts that must have kept him going when all felt lost. When he'd met her some years after the war ended, he let her read them, and she had, several times. So, she knows them. Knows the handwriting, the addresses, knows how the stamps curl, and the shape of every stain gathered from the trenches.

But... she doesn't know this one. It's newer. It's clean. And it's addressed to Maggie.

53

NOW

'Franny and I had an argument. It was stupid. She refused to believe that what I said happened at the grave actually happened. I think it was her belief that Mr Roberts had a "thing" for me, and me for him. So, she thought I either made it up, or took part willingly. Whichever way, she was very much anti-me that day. Childish stuff, really. I know she regrets that very much.'

Maggie is back in Taylor Clarke's office. Mid-June sun is creeping through his half-shut blinds, and though it's in Maggie's eyes, she likes the warmth of it and the way the lines of light look across the office.

It's clear from the way Taylor is looking at her – with his head on one side and his pen resting on his bottom lip – that this is one of the days when he doesn't speak much at all. It's these days that are the most dangerous for Maggie, because she always fills the silences, which she supposes is what he intends. Clever bloody therapists.

'When it came to going back to the camp, Franny wasn't talking to me, so she had her tea with Tracey Thornton and Carole Cassidy, who were the popular girls we hated in our year. She was doing it to piss me off, so I tried to ignore it. But when it came to bedtime, she stayed with them, slept in their tent.

'I was okay to start with. I'm not afraid of the dark, or creepy-crawlies or anything. But I was reeling from what happened earlier, and by the time the camp had settled, and the quiet had set in, I needed my friend. I needed Franny, and she wasn't there.

'She wasn't there to protect me.'

54

THEN

The tent is cold without the added bulk of Franny's sleeping bag and the warmth of her breathing. Maggie will miss the sporadic but constant kick of Franny's feet. She's had sleepovers with her, and they also camped out once in Maggie's back garden, and she's the most fidgety person.

There are noises outside the tent, but these don't worry Maggie. Most of them are the sounds of a campsite made up of school kids settling down: sporadic petty squabbling; the occasional breaking of wind followed by hoots of laughter; shushing from the adults; the clatter of glass and metal as some teachers sneak a crafty beer and smoke outside on the camping chairs, which they aren't supposed to, but everyone knows they do and turn a blind eye.

There are infrequent animal noises too: birds, some unidentified mammal out in the scrub of trees. Maggie isn't afraid. What scares her the most is when she hears someone say 'Goodnight then, Jim. See you in the morning' and hears the reply 'Night. I'm just going to finish this and then I'll be turning in.'

Jim is James Roberts. Mr Roberts. The man who, earlier that

day, pushed her into the headstone of someone else named Margaret. The man who'd shoved her face into stone and rubbed parts of himself against her bottom and the top of her thighs, and who'd made her fall out with her best friend because the thing she told her he did was too awful and too amazingly gross and too incredible for her to believe.

It's coming up to midnight. Everyone is exhausted from the day and now some of the sounds are snores from various tents. Maggie pulls her sleeping bag like a cocoon around herself so only from her nose is poking out. She hopes, hopes, hopes he goes to his tent and settles for the night. But she knows that won't happen. She knows.

And she hears it: the riiiiiiip sound of the zip opening. She holds her breath and prays some sensory illusion is making it sound nearer than it is and it's another tent. But the ground seems to move beneath her, her sleeping bag trembles. Someone is in the tent. She smells beer and cigarettes, hears his breathing.

He's in here. What she always knew would happen is happening.

The twelve-year-old Maggie is an intelligent, aware person. She studies diligently, rarely goes off the rails unless you count water fights with Franny in her back garden, or jumping on the bed into the small hours when they're having a sleepover, and she's a thoughtful and considerate friend. She doesn't like to see people hurt or upset, because her dad had always told her that if you consider for just one second what a person in fear or pain feels like, you'll want that to stop for them. If not, that makes you a monster. She never really believed in monsters, but...

A monster is in her tent.

She hears the zip again as it's closed against the chilly outside air, and now a deep and rhythmic breathing is warming the inside. She hears a rustling and feels hands sliding up her legs from the outside of her sleeping bag.

She'll never be able to explain why she doesn't scream. There's a silence inside the tent that's heavy and thick like treacle, as if her ears are filled with it. And if she breaks it, what then? Will there be repercussions? Pain? Retribution?

The weight of the arms moving up are soon joined by the weight of a body; knees resting one either side of the snake that is her in the sleeping bag. She pulls it up over her head, breathing in the cloying air inside it. The person behind the weight starts to unzip the side, and before she knows it, her body is exposed to the cold. She squeezes her eyes tight, tight shut, not wanting to see anything. Her dad had always told her that the only monsters you need to be afraid of are those you can actually see, not the ones you imagine. If she keeps her eyes closed, maybe it won't be real.

But it's real. This monster that feels like a bear with rough whiskers and hot breath is in the tent, on top of her. She turns over onto her stomach, thinking this will stop it, but it doesn't. His weight is still there, and now her face is squashed into the sleeping bag on top of the hard cold ground. If she opens her eyes, she can see the pale blue of the inside lining and the cream cotton stitching.

Hands pull down her pyjama bottoms and underwear. His skin feels hot against hers, but the pain is even hotter. He puts one hand on the back of her head, pressing it down so she cannot cry out even if she tries.

But she doesn't try. Instead, she counts the cream stitches in the pale-blue lining of the sleeping bag, and by the time she reaches 105, it's over.

55

NOW

'Take a breather, Maggie,' Taylor says. He pulls a tissue out of the box and Maggie instinctively reaches for it, but it's not for her. She watches as he removes his glasses, and with shaking hands wipes them with the tissue.

She suddenly wonders: *Do therapists see therapists?* It's a weird thought to have, right at this point, but how else do they process all the terrible things they must hear on a daily basis? And she's guessing they have to remain impassive. Who wants a therapist that falls apart? But they're human.

'I'm okay,' Maggie says with a deep sigh. 'At least, I know I won't die or anything, and as more time goes by, I'll get further away from it. It's not as raw, not as – what's the word? – *distracting* as it was. But I also realised lately that I need to despatch it, send it on its way. I need to rid myself of it.

'I've not really talked about it much. I've told a couple of people, each one once or twice and then the conversation was over. I've never dwelled on it. Maybe I should've – my silence and reticence to open up certainly ruined one of the most important relationships of my life.'

'Paul,' Taylor Clarke says, and Maggie nods.

'Yeah, Paul. My goodness, he was a fantastic man. Is, I should say. He's not dead! He's still very much alive and I see him from time to time.'

'You're still friends?'

They're more than that. They can never be any less than what they always were. She loves him deeply and he loves her.

But they can never be together, and she's always known that.

56

THEN

Maggie insisted Franny leave her to take the wedding decorations down herself, and somehow managed to persuade her to go so she could be alone with her thoughts. She's in her flat, tugging at balloons and banners, and piling them in a heap in the middle of her living-room carpet.

This is a nightmare she feels she'll never wake up from. And to top it all, Paul is on his way over after a very fraught telephone conversation. At first, she'd wanted to ignore his calls, hide away, definitely not talk to him. But she owes him an explanation. Yesterday he was her fiancé, living in her flat, waiting to go to his wedding. And then she'd pulled the rug away, and he'd had to come and fetch his stuff from the flat when everyone had been at The Cage eating the buffet that couldn't be cancelled, while Maggie cried under the duvet in her old room at her mum's.

By the time he arrives, Maggie has scrubbed the mascara off her face along with the black streaks of crying scars. Paul looks dreadful and as he passes her into the flat, Maggie wants to pull him into a hug, but she resists as it wouldn't be appropriate.

'I'm so sorry,' is the first thing she can think of to say, but it's trite and meaningless to this man. He looks broken.

'I don't want to hear anything by way of explanation, Maggie,' he says after flopping down onto the couch. He looks as though all the bits that make up his insides have been scooped out of him. 'What I want to hear is why you didn't feel you could be honest with me before today. I told you, I'd always listen and be there for you, but you had to tell me.'

'I know, Paul. I...'

'No, you don't know. You can't. Otherwise, we wouldn't be here now. We'd either be married, or you'd have spoken to me way before we got to this point. Way before we arranged a wedding.'

'I'm so sorry. I can't explain it.' Maggie's stomach and heart are fighting inside her body, and she's not sure if she's going to throw up or have a heart attack. 'Maybe I don't feel I deserve you.'

'Bullshit!' Paul shouts. Maggie flinches. She's never seen him angry with her before. With his father, when he's told her the stories about him. But never with her. 'Bull fucking shit. You know, without doubt, I hope by now, that I consider you my absolute equal, my soulmate, whatever that fucking means, and as far as I'm concerned, nothing that happened to you was your fault. You're an amazing person, and all that shit in the past means nothing in terms of who you are.'

'But it does, Paul, it does. It makes me the person who is still grieving for her dad. It makes me the person who had the unthinkable happen to her. It makes me the person who lost everything, and gave everything, and had everything stolen.'

'But who is still amazing and incredibly strong...'

'No, not strong. Not able to cope.'

She knows he doesn't want to hear it, but it's true. She's reached her limit.

'I can't drag you down with me anymore. You deserve better.'

'Don't say that.' Paul tries to touch her, hold her, but she moves away from him, backing towards the door. 'I can help you.'

'But we agreed I didn't need you to help me, right? I don't need you to save me.'

'For fuck's sake, Maggie. Why can't you allow me to help you? I'm not "anyone". I'm me. I'm Paul. I'm the man who loves you more than anything. I'm your partner, your equal. To refuse my help and my love is a fucking insult. I don't want to save you, for fuck's sake. I want to help you save yourself.'

'I just...'

'No! No excuses or bullshit. If you can't let me in, then it's your choice to be left alone. Yesterday was our wedding day, and you left it right until the last minute to decide this isn't for you. That we aren't for you. So, okay, have it your way. Be alone.'

Maggie doesn't want to be alone. But she has no control over this. It's too far ingrained and her mind is too messed up.

With Paul she's gone too far in one direction – away from him – to ever come back.

'I'm sorry, Paul,' she says.

And she really is.

57

NOW

'So that was the end, that night?' Taylor asks. He's made them a coffee and they're both clutching their mugs with two hands like it's twenty degrees below zero outside.

'It was awful. I've never been so keenly aware in all my life of hurting someone so grievously. If you were to take a puppy into a yard and kick it until it was dead, it would be the same feeling. I felt it in my gut, this horrible, incredibly deep sensation of being hurtful. And yet, I couldn't stop it. All I could think about at the time was the fact I needed to be alone, to wallow in whatever it was I needed to wallow in. And even looking at Paul and seeing how crippled he was, didn't stop me.

'He left, and I let him.' Maggie sips her coffee and is silent for a moment. She can still remember as if it was yesterday, the way he looked at her on his way out the door. 'I've never been as low as I was that night. I thought it was the end.'

'And was this the night you...?' He let the words drift away, not allowing the unthinkable, the unspeakable, out.

'Yes. It was the night I tried to kill myself.'

58

THEN

It's four in the morning when Maggie looks at the clock. The red digital display is wavering because her eyes are watery and stinging.

She's immediately disoriented because she doesn't remember coming to bed. This is scary. Her stomach and throat are really sore, and somewhere deeper inside, there's a twinge of something that's a mix of regret and fear. How did she get here? Why is there something niggling at the very core of her? She's never been so out of it drunk she couldn't remember what happened the night before.

She certainly remembers the day: her wedding day that never was. And Paul. God, how she'd hurt him. The look on his face as he'd left.

She hears a movement in the next room and is startled. Then, slowly, it starts to come back. Wine, lots of it. Diazepam, too much of it. Regrets, pain, memories, never-ending streams of both. Paul may not have been able to understand it, but there was far too much turmoil inside her for her ever to be of any use to him.

She remembers her gramps is here. Eighty-seven years old

and he's the one who came and held her up, helped her eject all the poison she'd drunk and swallowed, put her to bed. There's a bucket by the side of her bed, she discovers, as she puts her feet on the floor and almost knocks it over. Thankfully, it's empty.

Wincing from the pain in her head, she gets up and puts on a dressing gown. In the living room, her granddad is lying on the sofa – which is a sight to behold because he's over six feet tall and his legs are hanging over the edge. He's obviously not slept; his eyes are wide open and the blanket he's pulled from the airing cupboard is too small and his legs are wrapped around it. As Maggie walks into the room, he says: 'God Almighty, but you're a sight for sore eyes.'

'I see you haven't got your glasses on, Gramps,' Maggie says, and thinks this will make him smile, but it doesn't. His face is the most serious she's ever seen it.

He makes breakfast and they sit at her table by the window, looking out at the drizzly weather that seems appropriate for the mood and occasion. Maggie tries not to think that today she and Paul would've been heading off to Edinburgh for their honeymoon. A lovely B&B that she realises she forgot to cancel.

'I'm so very sorry for last night, Gramps,' Maggie says at last. 'I'm sorry you had to see it, to be there.'

'I'm incredibly relieved I was. Heaven knows where we'd be now if I'd not been. I can't bear it.' He reaches across the table and puts his hand over hers. 'You have to promise to tell me if you feel so low again.'

Maggie closes her eyes, takes a deep breath.

'I always feel like that, Gramps.'

She watches the pain cross his face, sees him wince. He's old and frail, and yet he's jumped in a taxi and come to help her. The guilt is overwhelming.

'But I promise I'll tell you. I won't let it get this bad again.'

'It's all my fault, Maggie. I'm so sorry. It's my fault.'

'Of course it's not,' Maggie says, horrified at the way he's tortured. 'It's no one's fault.'

Her granddad's hands shake as he drinks his coffee, and Maggie sees something flash in his eyes, like he wants to say something but can't quite get it out.

59

NOW

Simon received the email from 23andMe two days ago, but he hasn't had a moment to himself since then. He'd been on the tram when it came in, with a weirdly strangled version of the notification that accompanied his emails, and he'd only really seen the subject line: *We have Good News! DNA Results (Simon Goodwin) Ref 140395*

His heart had flipped, and he'd been about to hit the mail icon when the tram had juddered to a halt with some ceremony and much tutting and cursing from the passengers. So, he hadn't read it. He hasn't been able to stop thinking about it, but in a perverse way, he's not had the strength or courage to open it.

He thinks if they found nothing, he'll have to resort to Plan B, which he isn't relishing. He'll have to ask his mum all kinds of things, and she's not a woman who takes kindly to interrogation.

'Your dad is always giving me twenty questions about everything I do,' she often tells him. 'Like "What's for tea? Which supermarket are you going to? What are we watching tonight?" It drives me bonkers.'

She's not a woman with much patience, so he doesn't want to test its limits.

'You look, I can't,' he says to his best mate, Archie. They're in Wetherspoons for pre-pre-drinks before heading to the next pub for pre-drinks with the rest of the gang. Simon wanted to start the evening with just the two of them because he hasn't told anyone else about the DNA thing. 23andMe don't promise a result you'll be happy with; there's always a chance of disappointment. He doesn't want anyone around if he's disappointed.

Devastated more like.

He doesn't know what to expect. He's hoping there'll be some relatives out there, but he knows the trauma finding them could bring up. He's read the horror stories. People who meet the person they've been longing to meet for so many years, only to find they're a class A arsehole, or a sociopath. He doesn't know how he'd cope with that. He's not expecting to find her, but someone. Anyone.

Archie takes his phone from him and hits the email icon.

'Dude,' he says, 'you have no emails.'

60

THEN

On the morning after her suicide attempt, Maggie looks for the bear but can't find it. She wants to find it. Needs to. Because if anything is going to make sense again, especially the thought of her granddad being the most terrified she's ever seen him, she needs to know it was the bear that did it; the bear that made her do it.

But he's not around. He shrank away when Paul turned up to find out why his bride-to-be hadn't shown up at the church, and why she'd ripped out his heart. Maggie had wanted to tell him it was the bear – the bear, damn it – but the culprit was nowhere to be seen, and so she'd had to shoulder all the blame herself, and Paul had gone away not understanding anything.

It's still not here, so she can't explain anything to her granddad. She looks in her wardrobe, in her cupboards, under her bed, but the flat is empty of wild beast and full of concerned human. Her granddad's aura is one of heightened alarm. He watches her drink her coffee. He watches her eat her toast. He scans her face for anything, any sign.

When their breakfast is finished and Maggie has finally

persuaded him she won't try to hang herself with her dressing-gown belt, her granddad leaves, but says he'll phone her later.

As soon as she closes the door behind him, Maggie hears a low sonorous rumbling from behind her bedroom door.

Fucking typical.

61

THEN

Simon's in two minds about whether to do it. He's not a discontented individual and, in fact, is incurably happy. His childhood was nothing but joy and music and laughter, and his parents are insanely beautiful souls. He doesn't want for anything, either materially or emotionally.

But he's looking at a website that promises to help him find out who his birth parents are. His finger hovers over the "send" button on an application form that will essentially change his life. Does he want it to change? He doesn't think so. But he's waited eight years after sending his letter and getting no response.

His parents had told him the life-changing news on the morning of his eighteenth birthday, and he'd kind of known something was coming. They'd both been in strange moods since getting up, and his mother had been a bag of nerves. At the breakfast table she'd produced a letter from her apron pocket.

'Simon, love,' she'd said, and he could see her hands shaking. 'We promised we'd give you this on your eighteenth.'

She passed over a letter in a pale blue envelope. He could

see the writing on it was a child's writing, like it hadn't yet discovered itself or its form.

'What is it?' he asked.

'It's from your real mum, love.'

His real mum? Simon thought he'd misheard. 'What? Who?'

'A young girl, only a child herself. She went through a really tough time,' his mum said. She sat beside him at the table, instinctively pushing a hair back from Simon's face. She could see in his expression a million questions, and said she was prepared to answer them all – as many as she could, anyway. She knew the girl had been of school age and it had all been hushed up. But it was time to tell Simon what she knew.

Simon had opened the letter, which had already been opened eighteen years ago.

Dear Son,

I don't know if you'll ever read this, but I hope one day you might. In case you're wondering, I'm your mum. I'm only young, maybe much younger than you'll be when you get this, and that means you can't stay with me. If it were my choice, and if I could think of a way, I'd never let them take you. But I don't have a choice. I hope the place they're taking you to is really nice, with a good mum and dad.

One of the social workers said he'd make sure you get this letter when you're old enough, but I don't think I trust him. But I have to take the chance and hope he does what he says.

I hope you have a nice yard to play in. We've a big yard here, with borders of flowers. My dad, your granddad, loved gardening, and he always kept it so nice, but he's gone now, so it's kind of grown over with dandelions and daisies, which I think looks really nice, all those colours together, but mum, your gran, keeps saying one day she'll rip them all out and throw weedkiller down. Hopefully your yard, or maybe huge garden if you're really lucky, will have a lawn for you to kick a ball on, and maybe a swing set. I always wanted one of those.

Your granddad always believed if you wanted something badly enough, and if you worked really hard for it, you'd get it. If you prayed hard enough, God would help you. I don't believe that's true, the God bit, but I'm going to try and believe that one day, you and I will meet again. It might not be for a really long time, but I'm going to believe it will happen.

My love always,
Your mum xx

When he read that letter, he'd barely been an adult. His mum had answered as many of his questions as she could: a young schoolgirl, thirteen years old, who'd been through a very tough time. He'd tried to imagine it, but couldn't. He was eighteen and to him, a thirteen-year-old girl was a child. How could it happen? But he knew it did, all the time. Young girls had young boyfriends. Accidents happen. He wrote her a letter, but it had been full of confusion and not much hope.

After her initial verbosity and willingness to tell him all she could, his mum closed up – shut up shop. He tried to find out more, but she seemed hurt, sometimes asked him why he was not content with how things were. He knew she was afraid of losing him, so he let it pass, let the subject drop.

He's twenty-three now and time has moved on. The utter shock left him years ago, and he's resigned himself to the fact that the letter never reached her.

But technology and science are going to help him find her. Surely that'll work. They can do wonders these days.

He sends the email. Now all he can do is wait, and he'll figure out all the rest in due course.

62

NOW

'What do you mean, there are no emails? I have tons of them.'

Simon snatches his phone back from Archie, thinking he's kidding. But when he looks at the screen, he sees he's right. There are no icons at all, just a blank background. This is getting beyond a joke. No contacts either, so he can't phone anyone to find out what the email said.

When he gets to work, he googles 23andMe – thank goodness Google is still working on his computer – and finds their phone number. It takes ages to get put through to the right department, presumably because the phone systems are playing up, and when he is, what he hears isn't good.

'I'm so sorry, Mr Goodwin, but we've lost all the data in our database.'

'What do you mean? You have my results though, don't you?'

'We did have them, of course, and our computer generated your email, but we cannot access any information at the moment.'

'Do you know when you'll get the system back up?' Simon can feel a headache coming.

'It's not so much that the system is down, Mr Goodwin. It's that the database that contains all our files is empty. Everything has been wiped out. There's no data in the DNA database. Worldwide.'

Simon feels as though he's going to pass out. He's put all his hopes and energy from the last eight years into finding out this information. He was so close to knowing.

And now it's all been snatched away.

63

NOW

'What happened immediately after the rape? The day after?' Taylor asks.

Maggie jolts. Rape? It's incredible, but she's never given it that name in her head, or vocally after she told her mother, Franny, Paul. She always thinks of it as "the thing that happened" – when she thinks of it at all. She usually just pushes it away. Is "rape" what everyone else sees it as but her?

'I'm sorry, I don't mean to be so blunt...'

'No, that's fine,' Maggie says. 'I guess I've never really looked at this in any detail before. It's just been there, at the back of my head most of the time. And I know it's affected my life, because, duh, therapy... but it's weird when I hear you ask it like that.

'The day after, I guess I was numb. Was I numb? Yeah, I suppose I was. And also stunned, and pissed off with Fran, and in denial, at least at first. I didn't want anyone to know. I just wanted everything to be like normal.'

'It's not unusual to feel that way,' Taylor offers. 'Shutting down after such a traumatic event is a self-defence mechanism. It's a temporary solution, however.'

Maggie knows this. The feeling of numbness was just a transient thing and was quickly replaced with the enormity of the incident, and this had overwhelmed her for far too long.

But that day, the morning after, it had been like nothing had happened at all.

64

THEN

No one will ever know. She'll take the secret with her to her grave. She sees Franny over by the breakfast campfire, stirring beans in a saucepan and laughing with the enemy, who are Tracey Thornton and Carole Cassidy. She wants to go over and tell Franny how much she missed her in the tent, and how her not being there has changed the course of her whole life, but of course she doesn't, because something about the way Franny is acting with the girls makes Maggie think that wouldn't go down well. She didn't believe her about the graveyard, so goodness knows what will happen if she tells her about the tent. And besides, she wants to bury it as far down inside herself as it'll go, and maybe if she does that, it'll never have happened at all.

She eats breakfast by herself, a little way away from everyone else, and although the beans stick in her throat and she feels she'll never finish them, she does, and starts to feel a bit better. Eventually, Franny comes over and tells her she's sorry about the stupid argument, and about sneaking off with the dumb girls they both hate. They hug and get on the bus together. Franny gives her a tin of aniseed sweets she'd picked up in the little Wasdale shop they'd been at the day before.

Maggie knows how much Franny loves aniseed, so the gesture is sweet and touching.

They share the sweets on the journey, laughing and joking with the other boys and girls like any ordinary day. Mr Roberts doesn't come anywhere near.

When she gets home and goes up to her bedroom, Maggie puts the empty tin in her memory box, and when she shuts the lid, all is quiet.

65

NOW

'You've done some good work here today, Maggie. Do you feel you have?'

Maggie looks around the office, blinking. She feels as though she's been in a cave, not just physically but mentally for the past goodness knows how long. Taylor calls it good work, but she's not sure how to feel. Everything is happening all at once, it seems. Her business deal, which is great but, boy, it's been hard; her granddad dying, which is profoundly sad despite it being inevitable; her mother playing up this week, which she could do without; Paul phoning; her date on Friday, which she's up and down about – she could cancel but that would mean another usual boring night in with *EastEnders* and a bad curry from the local takeaway; the funeral; the bloody technology outages that have robbed her of many of her precious things.

And now, all this: this progress in her therapist's office. He thinks they've turned a corner and are on the home straight, she can see that. But there are a few more fences yet. She is, however, exhausted.

He says, 'I believe the only item left in the box is the bracelet, Maggie.'

'Not today, please. Can we leave that until tomorrow?'

She knows the bracelet is going to be the hardest one. It may well be the one that breaks her.

66

THEN

Every day is like an express train speeding past; one of those that doesn't stop at the station. The sound is like screeching and whistling, and sirens warning to keep behind the yellow line, step back from the platform edge. Stay away from danger.

But it's too late because she already stepped over, and fell. Fell pregnant. And when it happened it was like hands on her back, roughly pushing her off the platform. The hands of someone with ugliness inside who shoved her to land on cold steel and jagged gravel and a track that leads to nowhere good.

Someone who put one hand over her mouth and the other on parts of her she'd still not touched herself.

Her body now presents pain to her every day in different forms, like specials on a menu. Cramps in her pelvis, aches in her back, the sting of infection when she goes for a wee. She knows this won't be the worst pain she'll ever feel. That's to come. The agony of birth, the agony of physical separation, the agony of a love she doesn't want.

She can't stand the smell of Coca-Cola anymore. It used to be her favourite drink but now it makes her nauseous. But she'd kill to be able to stomach a Coke. Kill not to have to think about another life inside her. Kill to be the child she is, without having to worry about the arrival of another.

But at night she sleeps on her back, terrified of doing harm. Terrified of being the first person to hurt this life yet to come. She doesn't know how long it'll be before she can no longer avoid the truth. She's terrified of revealing it, and yet terrified to keep the secret inside her.

When she's five months gone, she's awoken by the sound of the radio blaring out downstairs and her mother warbling along to it. The smell of cinnamon is nauseating. Maggie can't bear it. Maybe there's some connection between cinnamon and Coca-Cola that makes them repugnant to her now. She struggles out of bed and slips on her dressing gown, pads down the stairs in her bed-socked feet.

She finds her mum in the kitchen. There's flour all over the table and all over her mum's face, and she's pulling and pushing violently at a huge mound of dough, stretching it out so it looks like when Maggie helps her wind her knitting wool. She's making her signature cinnamon rolls. Maggie wants to vomit.

'Ah, you're up at last,' her mum says, and pushes a strand of hair back, leaving flour in it. 'I was beginning to think you'd died up there.'

'It's Saturday, Mum. I'm tired.'

'You always seem to be tired lately. What's wrong with you?'

Maggie shrugs. She doesn't think her mum would like the truth about why she's always tired. She didn't believe her about what happened. But then, maybe this will prove it. She tugs gently on the dressing-gown belt – it's straining anyway – and it falls open. Her swelling belly, clothed only in a thin cotton nightdress, is now out there unconcealed. It's a relief to finally set it, and herself, free.

She stands at the door patiently, not moving until her mum's eyes finally open.

67

NOW

After the therapist and work, Maggie is at her gran's house. Dorothy wanted her to pick up the crocheted blanket. Maggie could do without this because she's drained after her session with the therapist, and all she wants to do is get in the bath with a glass of wine and some Shostakovich and forget everything. This week is turning out to be too much.

While her gran is fussing in the kitchen making tea and arranging a month's supply of biscuits on a plate, Maggie has to sit down suddenly, taken over by the weight of it all. It's not like she's a stranger to grief and loss, but it all seems much heavier when you realise everything and everyone is getting older, nearer the end of whatever passes for a life.

The blanket is folded up on the armchair her granddad always sat in and Maggie looks at it forlornly. She misses her gramps keenly. She can't believe she can't just walk into the next room and talk to him, like she has every other day for the whole of her life. She wonders how you're supposed to cope when something like this happens, when a part of you is cut away, like an amputated limb or the surgical removal of an organ. Most organs that are removed are replaced, or else they weren't vital, like a gallbladder. But what about when your heart is removed?

This is how Maggie feels. Her heart has been ripped out without anaesthetic.

'Here we are, love.' Her gran puts a tray on the table. Maggie takes a biscuit, even though she doesn't really want one, because this is what she has to do when her gran offers one. There are no ifs, ands or buts. The second it's in her mouth, the sweetness of the custard cream transports her to a place where everyone is present: her mum and dad, her gran and gramps. A place and time when everything was simple. When her childhood was uncomplicated and she was yet to see anything bad. A time before everything, when everyone was young, and healthy, and together.

'Oh, love,' her gran says, seeing her pain. 'He wouldn't want you to be sad for him.'

'I know, Gran. I'll be okay.' Would she though?

They drink the tea and eat the biscuits, in silence for a while as the absence of her granddad fills the room around them.

Then her gran breaks the silence with something Maggie can't believe she's hearing.

'I found a letter in your gramps's box, Maggie. It's to you, from Charlie.'

Hearing his name is like an electrical jolt. She reaches for the envelope and sees it's dated 2013.

'I don't understand.' She turns it over in her shaking hand, looks at her gran.

'I know, it's mad. And I'm sorry, but I only found yesterday. I'd no idea he had it. Your mum must have given it to him.'

Her mum? Maggie can't believe her mum would keep this

from her, that her gramps would keep it from her. A letter from Charlie.

Her Charlie.

Maggie doesn't speak for a long time. She tries to think back to when she was thirteen, which seems like a lifetime ago and yesterday at the same time.

68

THEN

They're in the corner of the room, whispering. Maggie can't hear what they're saying, but she can imagine it as if she's there among them.

'For the best.'

'In the interest of the child's welfare.'

'Too young.'

'She'll see it's the right thing, soon enough.'

She's heard them say all these things before, and they say them easily, like the decisions being made now will be effortless to stick to. But how will it be easy to never see him again? He's part of her. He came from her. He's clinging tightly to her finger and attaching himself like a limpet to her breast. He needs to feel her touch and to hear her voice because it's the only way he'll know the world is safe; she feels this instinctively.

If her voice and her touch go away, who'll keep him from harm? Who'll come when he cries? Who will feed him?

The whispering stops, and it's the scariest silence.

69

NOW

If the light had been on, she'd be able to see the bear, so Maggie is relieved it's dark. The smell of its breath is bad enough without having to see the saliva dripping from its mouth. Over the last few weeks, puddles of dribble have become more frequent and greater in number, and she doesn't want to deal with that now: the stickiness of it, the feel of the spit under her soles and between her toes as she makes her way to the bathroom for a pee.

She's tried to remove the puddles and the stains they leave but no matter how hard she scrubs, they never come out.

Taylor Clarke told her – while she was staring out of his window at the rain lashing and the branches of the tree smacking the glass like it was a naughty child – that delusions and hallucinations can be a symptom and direct result of childhood trauma, including but not limited to sexual abuse. When he'd said that, he'd raised his right eyebrow ever so slightly.

She'd wanted to say *No shit, Sherlock* but held her tongue.

Seeing the therapist is making the bear sightings more frequent but also, ironically, makes her believe they'll soon become much less. Now she's finally getting it all out and has actually talked about the rape – it's still hard to call it that – the anxiety is reducing. She feels *heard* for the first time in many years. Although she's told people some of what happened, she's never laid it all out.

Like a jigsaw puzzle she's piecing together, she's laid out all the borders of the sky and now she's working on the scene in the middle. If she can fit the last few pieces in, the jigsaw will be complete.

She goes to bed dreaming of that piece of the puzzle. And it has Charlie's face on it.

70

NOW

The next day when she wakes, Maggie is desperate to see her therapist and is thankful she booked a session for every day this week. Today, she's also meeting Paul for a drink with his two sons. She doesn't feel she can do that unless she's expelled at least some of the breath she's been holding in since her gran gave her the letter.

She tries to explain it to Taylor, but she's rambling and doesn't blame him when he asks loads of questions to clarify.

'Last night, your gran gave you a letter? I can see from your demeanour it was an important one. Who was it from?'

'Charlie. My Charlie.'

'I'm confused. Who's Charlie?' Taylor flips back through pages of his notebook, as if waiting for the name to jump off the page somewhere in Maggie's case history. 'I don't recall you mentioning him.'

Maggie flops down on the couch and puts her face in her hands. 'Charlie is my son,' she says.

71

THEN

Maggie doesn't think she can do it. Her body seems melded to his and she can feel the distant pulse of his heart. His life. The harder and closer she holds him the stronger that pulse is. It stands to reason that if she lets go, loosens her hold on his tiny body, her link to his heartbeat will be lost. A nine-month plus three-week bond severed with one disconnective movement.

'It's time,' the social worker – one of a team of three who've ripped her life apart – says. This one has pale grey hair and pale grey skin and pale grey clothes, and is male, and has probably never held a baby close to his chest. Has definitely never carried one in his uterus or pushed one out of his vagina. She knows all the proper words for everything because they did it in biology not long ago.

But he has the authority to take her baby away. Because her mum has given it to him and Maggie has no say in it. No say whatsoever.

She has no say in anything. Never has. No say in having sex, no say in getting pregnant, no say in giving birth. She has no voice at all. She's too young, and too innocent, and too vulnerable, and everything is just too overwhelming.

Inside her is a silent scream only she can hear. When she looks at her mother and pleads with her eyes, she doesn't see, doesn't hear and doesn't care. She's never forgiven Maggie for being a trollop. She's never believed it wasn't some random boy. She's never believed about him, about what happened.

So, the little heartbeat moves away – is wrenched away – and in its place a coldness settles. She watches as Mr Pale Grey hands her son over to another of the social workers, and then they all leave the room. Except her mum, who busies herself gathering all the things from the cot: soft yellow blanket, plush rabbit, farmyard animal mobile. When her arms are full, she leaves the room.

The cot is empty.

Everything is empty.

Except her heart, which will never be empty of love. And her breasts, full of milk and still sore from his last feed minutes ago.

72

NOW

'My goodness, Maggie, I'm sorry. That must've been so traumatic for you. It's a lot to carry around with you all these years on top of everything else.'

This morning, the coffee is not hitting the spot. Maggie needs something stronger. She shoots a look at the clock. Just a couple of hours to go before she meets Paul.

'Yeah, it was. It's surreal though. Over the years I started to think about it as though it had all happened to someone else. It was the best way to deal with it. But... I think that's what got me into all the trouble I've had with everyone. My mum, Paul, even Franny at times.'

Is it this simple? Maggie thinks. You come to a therapist, you talk about the things you kept hidden inside yourself for years, and you come out of it feeling better. Just like that. Like a miracle happened. *It can't be this easy, surely.*

But it does seem to be. For the first time in as long as she can remember, she feels a tiny chink in the chain-mail curtain of anxiety. The memories that she'd suppressed for so long are being exposed as imposter-monsters. That was her gramps's word. Imposter-monsters are those things your mind gives great size, power and strength to when you aren't even capable of looking at them. It's as though they know. They know you won't look at them or face them, so they have the confidence to shout as loud as they like and to roar like a lion rather than squeak like a mouse. Like the bogeyman in the wardrobe or under the bed, or the Wizard of Oz who turned out to be a fraud and had no power at all.

Letting go of fears is the secret, she realises. Being brave enough to say all the words and cry all the tears so all the power of the monster is spent.

And to talk about the painful things.

Like the bracelet.

73

THEN

Her mum has dropped something on the floor. It's lying under the empty cot. From her bed, she can't make out what it is and she hurts too much to move. The birth had been arduous and painful, her young body unable to cope, and the last three weeks have been tough.

Sleep has eluded her for many reasons – not the least of which has been having a tiny human clamped to her breasts at all hours of the day and night – and she's exhausted. Everything feels like a dream; the room is always wavering like she's underwater and her eyelids are heavy lead shutters. Sometimes, she can imagine it is all a dream and that none of it actually happened.

Not the horror of getting pregnant, not the terrifying changes in her body, not the shock of pushing a person out of her at age thirteen. But she knows it's not a dream and that it happened, because she sees the shock on her mother's face. She looks like someone who went to sleep one night in one life, and woke up the next day in another – like she's been taken to an alien planet and she doesn't know how everything works. The others, the social workers, their look is more snootiness than shock, as though they've seen it countless times and nothing rocks their world anymore. They look at her as if she's something dirty that needs to be cleaned up.

And now everything is clean. Once the cot is dismantled and her breasts stop producing and leaking, there'll be no evidence he ever existed.

But that thing, under the cot, she realises what it is now. It's the tiny powder-blue plastic bracelet the hospital had put on Charlie that the grey-faced social worker had cut off before they took him from the room. She can't let anyone clean it away; it's the only thing left.

Ignoring the pain deep in her stomach and lower down where they stitched her, she gets out of bed and picks up the bracelet. The room spins and she has to sit back down quickly until it stops, but she has the bracelet hidden tightly in her fist. That the social worker discarded it the way he did rips something inside her apart. *My boy isn't disposable*, she thinks.

'Baby Boy Milburn', she knows it says without looking.

'Charlie,' she whispers into the room. After her dad. It's a secret she can never share with anyone.

'Don't name him,' her mother had warned. 'It's not your place to.' But she can say it when no one is here, before she hides it inside forever.

'Charlie, Charlie, Charlie,' she chants into the emptiness, until she hears her mother coming back up the stairs to take the cot.

She hides the bracelet inside her nursing bra, next to the last place he was.

That night, she dreams of her father in the depths of a fevered sleep. She wishes he was here to cuddle her and warm the place in her heart that's been vacated so abruptly and cruelly. But he isn't here. Maggie feels it deep in her bones, in her organs, in her skin and hair. The absence of her father.

No one really knows what profound loss is like until the moment they experience it, and Maggie has felt it three times. Once when she lost her dad to the cancer that ate him slowly away, once when her innocence was ripped from her and she had no one to help her, and now, when her beautiful boy is being taken away.

If he'd been here, her dad would've fought those social workers away like a gladiator fights lions. In fact, it would never have got this far, because he'd have fought her mother. Maggie has no doubt about that. He was always her greatest champion. He'd have believed her about Mr Roberts. He'd have hunted the man down and torn him apart, made him pay, made him suffer for what he did. And he'd have told Maggie's mum no one would be taking Charlie away. Told her that Maggie makes her own decisions, and that he trusts them to be right.

The only thing she can do to bring him here, to feel his presence, is to give her son his name. That way, another Charles Milburn will be walking the earth and she knows it'll be a richer world for that. Even if she'll never see him, she'll know he's out there. Always.

74

NOW

There's an emptiness inside Aaron Griffiths that's not unpleasant. A space, a gap, that was once filled with fear. He used to wake each day in a cold sweat of terror and uncertainty, but now when he opens his eyes first thing, there are several moments of stillness and quiet; a peace within his chest where before there was hammering. The terror was always about how many messages he'd have to deal with before even getting out of bed; little red dots of torture on the icon on his screen. The uncertainty was about how gruesome they'd be, and whether the threats in them would turn out to be real that day.

Today when he goes downstairs after taking his uniform off, his dad is whistling away to the radio. He loves having him and his brother staying with him and when they're not, he's probably lonely. He can't be used to the quiet. So, his whistling fills the little house with happiness and joy. Aaron feels it seeping into his bones. And they're off out for their tea in a bit, after meeting his dad's friend.

The radio is loud. The DJs are joking they've gone back to the Dark Ages and are having to put CDs on because the database of tunes that was always at their fingertips has gone.

The TV in the other room spews out cartoons and then the early evening news.

It's all normal. More normal than it's been for a while.

'Do you know, I love this,' his dad suddenly says, staring dreamily through the kitchen window. 'The songs. They sound so much better somehow. I guess it's like people who love vinyl always prefer that to CDs, because you can hear the dirt and fluff on the needle and that lovely crackle they make. And it's the same with CDs compared to sound files. There's something there, something solid and material. It's not just computer chips and soulless nothing.'

Aaron thinks his dad might be cracking up and he rolls his eyes then starts laughing.

'You seem happier,' his dad says.

'I am,' says Aaron, and he goes into the living room to torture his brother.

Simple pleasures.

75

NOW

Paul has brought Maggie to a Harvester in Didsbury, where workers are stopping by for drinks on their way back from the office and families are having an early tea. He talks to her about her granddad, Harold. When he was seeing Maggie, he always enjoyed visiting him. Somehow, they always ended up in Harold's shed with a few cans of beer and would chat until Maggie dragged Paul out.

'I can't believe he's gone, Mags. His light had always seemed so bright I thought it would never go out,' Paul says as they settle at the table with their drinks. After he and Maggie broke up, he carried on visiting for a while, until having his family got in the way. 'The funeral is quick. I can't believe it's this Saturday. You're lucky.'

'Yeah, I know. I think the priest is afraid of him.' Maggie laughs. 'He was almost a hundred and he went to church every Sunday without fail. I think they have a special fast track to Heaven for people like him.'

'I wouldn't be surprised. How are you?'

'Oh, you know, okay.' She really is, despite the emotional

session with Taylor Clarke. She feels drained and wrung out, but cleansed. 'Gramps was old. He was tired and was ready.'

'He was an absolute fucking legend is what he was. I'm glad you invited me to the funeral.'

'Of course! He loved you.'

'I really regret losing touch with him, but when you and I split and I met Louise and had the boys, it just became too hard to juggle. And... it was complicated because of you and me.'

His sons, Aaron who's just turned ten and George who's eight, are with him. Maggie looks over at them and feels a pull somewhere inside. She shrugs it away.

Paul looks so good that Maggie feels a twinge of something that's not quite regret because too many years have passed and she actually likes their new relationship. But there's something about him today. He's never had his sons with him before and this makes him look like a proper grown up. There's a throb of emotion that's sadness mixed with joy that they didn't work out but, boy, look at him now.

The fabulousness of him and the way he is with his boys makes Maggie miss her own dad and granddad more.

76

NOW

They're sitting in the beer garden and the sun is hot on their backs. They have tall glasses of lager with ice sweat dripping down the sides. His kids are running on the pub lawn, which is strewn with coloured plastic balls, toy cars, kiddie JCBs. Paul is constantly getting up, picking his boys up one by one and setting them the right way, wiping their noses as snot bubbles sprout and burst in their panting excitement. And he seems to love it. He seems so intensely alive it hurts Maggie's eyes to see it, like when you try to look at the sun and it burns an image into your retinas. Paul is the sun, big and proud as a god, and his sons are orbiting around him. And all Maggie can think is: *I missed my dad's youth. I missed seeing him seeing me.*

Paul's longish hair – like her dad used to wear his – is constantly flopping into his face, and he folds it back with a flat palm so it exposes his eyes, all sparkling and liquid with love and Maggie's mind races like a devil is chasing it and she thinks unstoppable heart-aching thoughts. *Dad was like that once; he was young and beautiful and full of love and joy, and I was too young to see it as I ran around his legs like a shark in a choppy sea he'd accidentally waded into, and he was there, present and alive, watching my fin circle him, and he embraced the heart-wrenching danger of it like I see Paul doing, and I think I realise now, through Paul, that dad was happy and proud and paternally rapturous, but this ankle-biter, this shark, stopped circling and swam to shore, to a life inland from the adventure, and he wanted to stay in the water, so he was out of reach, and I forgot to look at his floppy hair and sparkling eyes, or didn't realise I needed to, because soon it would be too late and he'd be gone across a cosmic ocean too wide and vast for all of us, gone completely, gone from life, and I look at Paul now, at his fabulousness, and I remember my dad's and it cuts me so deeply, so keenly, that I'll never have the chance to tell him just how fucking amazing he was.*

'You okay, Mags?' Paul places his hand over Maggie's and she breathes out deeply at last, expelling the air she's been holding. She doesn't know how to explain the feelings she's having; that her heart has just cracked open. 'If all this is too much today... I mean, you've been through the wars this week.'

'I'm okay. I'm just so aware that you never really remember the youth of your parents,' she says and then takes a long swig of lager to give her time to carry on. She needs the coolness of the drink to calm her and to swallow down the lump in her throat. 'You don't notice it, but when you look back you realise you knew them when they were in their twenties and thirties. Like you are, with your kids. It's staggering when you suddenly realise that.'

'Mags...' Paul's face is pulled into a look Maggie doesn't like. She hates sympathy, hates it when he worries, and Paul looks like he's heading there.

'Oh, I'm fine,' she assures him, but he doesn't look convinced. 'I just mean their youth passes you by and you're oblivious to it. You never remember seeing them young, with fresh faces and strong bodies. You never really think about them having hopes and dreams, and you never wonder if they came true. My dad never got old but my mum has, and I can't remember either of them in their prime because I was just getting on with being a child.'

She looks at Paul's kids: Aaron has smacked George in the face and George looks like he's going to scream but hasn't yet decided exactly when. Paul runs over, drags the two back, one wriggling protesting monster in each hand.

'This is kids, Mags!' he says with a mocked disgusted look. 'These snot-faced, filthy, murdering animals are kids. These are boys. And no wonder kids never think about or remember their parents' youth; they're far too fucking busy wrecking it and making you old before your time!'

Maggie snorts just as she's taking a drink and lager shoots up her nose.

'Paul!' she protests but she's laughing. Paul suddenly looks alarmed.

'Boys, there's no need to tell your mum about me using a bad word, okay? Keep schtum and you can have a milkshake at Macca's on the way home.'

And so it goes, thinks Maggie. *Families. Life. We wipe snot and we try to prevent injuries and death, and we bribe and we compromise and all the while, we love.*

'Hey,' says Paul with a wink. 'Imagine if *we'd* had them.' He stops suddenly in his tracks, seeing the look of pain that crosses Maggie's face. 'Oh fuck, I'm sorry. Stupid bastard.'

'No, it's not what you think.' She wipes a hand over her eyes. She doesn't want him to feel bad. 'I've... I've found him.'

She can't help her mouth moving into something she thinks might be a smile. But she's terrified also.

'Oh my God! Where? Who? When?' Paul stops as he's bending George into his coat, leaving him half in, half out.

'The day after Gramps died,' Maggie says and the relief of telling someone, at last, makes her burst into tears. 'Gran found a letter from him in his old wooden war box. So, I suppose you could say *he* found *me*. His name is Simon.'

77

THEN

Dear Mum (this is weird)

I found out about you two days ago. Before that I didn't know you existed and thought my mum and dad were my real parents. But when I turned eighteen, they decided it was time I knew about you. I have to be honest and say I don't know what to think. It'll take a while.

Part of me is angry that they kept your letter from me for so long, but another, more grown-up part, understands why; understands the fear they felt. I was obviously given up for a reason and I've no idea what that reason was, but they wanted to protect me from whatever it was I was taken away from. And also, they didn't want to lose me.

You say you were young. I won't pretend to understand the circumstances, but I hope you'll be able to tell me. I'd like us to meet and to talk about things.

Would you like that? Even after all these years? If that's still your wish.

In answer to your questions, I've had a really lovely life and live in a nice house with a garden. I love music and my dream is to one day own my own music shop, so I'm studying Business and Management at MMU – that's in Manchester.

This letter will go to the adoption agency and then back to you. I've enclosed all my details, our address and phone number. Maybe by the time you contact me, I'll have grown more used to this idea... that somewhere out there is the woman who gave birth to me.

I just keep thinking of all the lost time, and how you must have been thinking all this time that I'd chosen not to reply.

I hope to meet you very soon,

Simon x

78

NOW

Franny realises no two people really think the same way. They can be in the same ballpark, the same general area, but ideals are as unique as people.

When one person says they believe women and men are equal, *their* version of it can differ to another person's. Being equal may mean *capable* of making their own decisions, but not being *allowed* to.

It may mean they can go out to work like their partner but also mean they have to sacrifice their career – to have a family, for instance, or to just be there when the other gets home because they don't trust you – because they don't earn as much money, and for some reason the earning of money is crucial to the permitted degree of fulfilment in life.

It may mean they can explore their sexuality and needs in the bedroom in equal measure to their partner, but if one of them wants to try something painful and humiliating, the other one has no say in the decision and must agree without question, because 'a marriage is a marriage, and all needs must be met equally by both parties'.

Franny and Steve are eating dinner and *Coronation Street* is on the TV that's mounted on a bracket on the wall in the corner of the dining room. The noises are forks and knives tinkling and scraping on plates. The smells are beef casserole and the cigarette Steve always has on the go in the ashtray next to his plate. Every second or third mouthful of food is partnered with a drag. Franny finds this repulsive, but she must let him live his equal life. As he pointed out to her, she's quite welcome to smoke at the table too. Or shoot fucking heroin into her arm as far as he's concerned.

That's another thing about equality. You're allowed to do anything you want, even the abhorrent things you'd never do. Like drugs, which she doesn't, and alcohol, which she does but really wants to stop, and having the right to discipline your spouse, which he does and knows she doesn't have the balls to do.

Franny is nonplussed at the patriarchy – or rather the *uber-masculation*, which she's not sure is even a word but it should be – and the insults that fly her way on the nights they're discussing the equality of their life. She's told to *man up*, or *grow a pair*, as if being a man, and having testicles, is the standard to which all humans should aspire. When she's 'being unreasonable' about his sexual overtures and suggestions, she's a *cunt* and a *bitch*, and when she agrees to them, she's *a whore, a prostitute, a fucking sleazy alley cat who can't get enough dick*!

This kind of talk is what he does whenever he's heaving his disgusting body into hers, because it makes him King and it makes him hard. And she's a *fucking battle-axe twat* when she objects to him speaking in such a way. After he's finished, he laughs, lying on his back with his disgusting penis lying like a withered worm on his thigh. The memory of the feel of it burns into her.

She wants to block out the frightening noise in her head by finding out what the residents of a fictional TV street are up to.

There's always lots of stuff going on, and most of it is far-fetched, but it beats reality sometimes to have something ridiculous to focus on to give life balance. Steve calls it *stupid fucking women's shit*, but at the moment it's saving her life.

Steve wants to talk – again – about Franny giving up work, so she's given him extra meat and potatoes to give his jaw something else to do. She's also turned the TV up louder. She knows this is risky – ignoring him – so she's pulled her chair a little bit further away, out of reach of his arm length. Since it's summer, she wants to wear sleeveless tops and can't take any risks. The burn rings are only just fading.

'Why does Maggie need you?' he asks, and his words come out with a mouthful of smoke, which she swallows involuntarily with her beef. Here it comes. He hates that she has Maggie; hates all her friends and colleagues. If he had his way, she'd have only him.

'We're a great team. We're partners.' Franny's said these words more times than she can count. She pulls at her hair; the pressure on her scalp sends a soothing feeling into her stomach, quieting the acid in there.

'You're a *junior* partner,' he sneers, like this word is filth and she's not worthy of the one that comes after it. 'You put up a pittance to get in the door, and she won't miss you when you're gone.'

When?

Franny puts her knife and fork down. She remembers the octopus at the aquarium they went to recently, on a day he'd been in a good mood and hadn't hit her for eight hours. It had been clinging to the glass and then releasing itself, over and over like captivity and freedom were seamlessly and eternally intertwined. She'd envied its fluidity and grace.

Considered dangerous and yet capable of displaying intelligence, ingenuity and fierce love, the epithet on the side of the octopus's tank had read. She wonders why love needs to be fierce; why anything in life worth having must be fought for.

Her marriage isn't worth having, but her life... her life is worth fighting for.

'I'm leaving you,' she says, and she feels her suckers pulling away from the glass, her body undulating away into liquid light.

79

NOW

He looks ridiculous. Not that Maggie thinks she's anything to write home about herself, but this man is literally triangular. He looks like that cartoon character she used to love to watch in the nineties on MTV – Johnny Bravo. All square jaw and tapering torso with arms he can't place by his side. Her dad used to say of those kinds of bodybuilders that it looks like they're carrying two rolls of carpet all the time.

She watches him come across the room towards her and tries to paint her face with a welcoming smile. She thinks she's pulling it off until she sees uncertainty and fear flick across his face. She tries harder.

'Ben?' His smile answers her question.

'So good to meet you at last.' He extends a hand and takes hers; a disappointing, but not altogether surprising, limp-fish shake. Maggie suspects all his energy is zapped daily at the gym.

And with carrying those two rolls of carpet around all day.

'Maggie. Likewise. Do you have a drink?'

He's seen she has a drink, but she allows this nervous inanity. 'Yes, thanks. I'm good.' She notices he has a piece of toilet paper stuck under his chin, with a bloom of red at its centre.

He signals the barman over to the counter and orders a pint of Punk IPA and she watches him pull out his wallet from the back pocket of his tight jeans. She wants to see something in him she'll like, or could grow to like, but she's fazed by his shake and his height which, now he's right next to her, is too much. He'd said in his profile he's six-two, but she'd never envisaged what that means. What it looks like. Until now. And it doesn't look good against her five feet four. It looks like he's Arnie and she's Danny DeVito from *Twins*.

'So.' He flashes his ultra-white teeth at her. There are beads of sweat on his forehead and top lip and his jacket is far too tight. 'How's your day been so far? Busy?'

'Can't complain,' Maggie says. She hates this. Small talk. It'll be their journey here next, then the weather, and it'll move on to what box sets they're watching. She wishes she could fast-forward to the meal, to the walk to the taxi rank. To knowing if this is different or just like the rest. Just a waste of an evening and a new pair of tights.

She'd have cancelled last minute, but of course the dating app isn't working and she couldn't have stood him up. So, she's here, for better or for worse.

Within five minutes she realises it's just a waste of a new pair of tights.

80

NOW

Maggie hates so-called chivalry.

Back in the day, when she showed any signs of being upset, or sad, or lonely, her mum would always say: 'Don't worry. Someone will come along. You'll meet someone special.'

Her mum thought a man was needed for everything. Not just grouting the bathroom or putting out the bins, but for cheering, and propping, and *saving*.

Disney films were always about princesses being rescued by handsome princes and, yeah, Maggie has been guilty in the past of playing that princess and dancing around the bedroom singing 'Someday My Prince Will Come', but that was before she grew up. That was before her dad had finished raising her.

Now she's sinking and she knows a prince won't save her.

Her dad had thought differently to her mother. He would often say, 'Don't take any notice of that nonsense, darling. You don't need anyone but yourself. Remember that.'

And to her mum: 'Cynthia, stop filling her head with nonsense. You didn't need rescuing. I didn't rescue you.'

He'd told her men are often useless anyway, and a woman could do better than ever to rely on one.

'And you're strong, Maggie darling. You're my warrior. You make me proud every single day because I know that no matter what happens to you, you'll be fearless and you'll always be okay.'

She doesn't often feel okay, but she tries. For her dad, she always tries. And for her granddad.

She's in Wetherspoons and she's talking to her latest swipe right, Mr Triangular, and although she can see his lips moving, she can't hear anything. She stopped listening when he told her she could absolutely not put her hand in her pocket. They've been to dinner – they had steak and two bottles of Malbec – and now he's refusing to let her pay for a poxy pint of beer in Spoons and she feels like she'll scream like a banshee if she opens her mouth.

So, she just smiles.

'How much do you make?' she asks, suddenly overcome with devilment.

'I'm sorry...?'

'Money, per year, how much?'

'I... er...'

'Ballpark. It's a valid question. For the point I want to make.'

The guy looks terrified, but this just spurs Maggie on. The more she thinks about it, the more furious she's feeling.

'Er... about... er... forty-five. But I'm just working my way up and...'

'I make eighty,' Maggie says and she enjoys the way he flinches at that. 'And that's just what I pay myself, because I have my own business. I pay my junior partner well too. If you'd even bothered to ask me about what I do, which you didn't because it's obviously more important to tell me all about what a *lion* you are in the boardroom, you'd know about my really successful business. But you didn't. You just assumed I'd enjoy being condescended to all night and having everything paid for.

I didn't enjoy that. I haven't had a meal I haven't paid for, or shared the cost of, in over ten years. I also like to buy a round of drinks when it's my turn. I live in a townhouse on the River Irwell, and my fridge is full of Veuve Clicquot.'

She's aware of how she sounds. Even to her own ears, this is cringeworthy. She hates women who are militant about this stuff. She's always thought *be independent by all means, but don't be an arsehole about it.* She firmly believes in that and lives by it.

But she's pissed off. She's had a bad week. She's grieving like a motherfucker. This guy is messing with the wrong person on the wrong day. And strangely, as if to underline her thought process, she can't stop thinking about Paul.

'I'm sorry. I shouldn't have come.' She puts her drink on the bar, stands up. She sees her date looks terrified, confused.

'It's not you, it's me,' she says and then snorts at the hilarity of the cliché. She feels hysteria building. 'My granddad just died. It's his funeral tomorrow. I can't do this.'

'Oh, I'm so sorry. You should've said earlier.'

'It's okay. Just... just stay and finish your drink. I'm sorry I wasted your time.'

All she wants now is to get home, open a bottle of wine and watch something mind-numbing on telly.

81

NOW

A blocked O *and Emergency Calls Only* has been at the top of Franny's screen for a few days, and she's got used to the fact that she can't call anyone, but now she needs to.

She presses 999 and waits for that voice. She's heard it before, when she's been hiding from one of his rages in the understairs cupboard with a busted bottom lip, which she told everyone who asked that it was from when she was opening a stupidly wrapped parcel from Amazon that had tons of tape on, and when she pulled hard at a stubborn bit her hand slipped and she smacked herself in the face. The police had come then and sat with her for a while, calming her, asking her if she needed to find somewhere to live, or if there was anyone they could call. She'd told them she was very sorry she'd wasted their time, maybe she was making too much of a fuss. She had no one to call, she said, which was the only reason she called them. She did have people. She had her mum and Maggie. But she could never call them about this.

And there was that time he was comatose upstairs after breaking one of her ribs. She got a ride in the ambulance that time, and he was taken to the police cells to sleep off the alcohol.

When he woke, he was interviewed but then they let him go. Afterwards, she told anyone who noticed that she'd been getting off the bus and the driver slammed on his brakes as she was walking up the aisle and she'd smacked her side into the hand bar with the bell on it.

Broken ribs are the worst things to heal because as they do the pain seems to get worse, and that makes it harder and harder each day to hide it, or fool people. And often, people knock into you accidentally, or you really do touch the hand bar on the bus and it's all you can do to stop from screaming. The last thing you want is to attract attention and have to go through the story again hoping you get it the same as the last time you told it.

Today, hitting 999 brings nothing but silence. She expected it but it still brings a shiver of unexpected emotions.

Defiance. Relief.

She could walk across the room and pick up the landline, because that's still working in this new and crazy world. But that would mean stepping over him. It would mean risking getting blood on her nice white trainers.

Her bag is by the front door, with no obstacle in the way. She stands and picks it up. Walks out without looking back.

82

NOW

Franny is out in the street, walking to the Eccles Metrolink stop nearby. The day is crisp and clear, as late summer days can be. The light is beautiful. But she hardly registers it. She can't breathe. She can't... She stops and leans against a wall.

She claws at her throat like she's trying to remove a tight scarf, but there's nothing there. Her body makes the movement of breathing – her chest hitches up and down – but nothing is going in or coming out. There is no air, nothing but silence.

It's like the time she inhaled a piece of beef when Steve had walloped her mid-chew. It had wedged in her windpipe and for several terrifying minutes she'd struggled for breath, pleading to him with her eyes to help, to get it out. To hit her again, please, this time on her back, or to do the Heimlich.

But he'd sat there, smoking, smirking, watching her as if she were a fish he'd just pulled from the water and he was looking at it flip and flop at the bottom of a boat. So, she'd struggled from her chair into the kitchen, remembering something out of nowhere – an episode of a drama she'd watched where someone had given themselves the Heimlich by walking fast into their kitchen worktop. It gave her a bruise under her ribs to add to the collection, and afterwards, as she gasped and cried, Steve came in and asked her what was for pudding and told her to stop snivelling.

Today, she's not choking on beef, but she's choking on her life. This time the Heimlich comes when she steps over him and walks out of the door, because she's ejecting him like a piece of meat from her throat. She has to trust this process: she left, she's leaving, she'll leave; past, present and future. Simple.

She feels that everyone on the tram is looking at her. Men sneering because they can see how worthless she is. Women pitying her because they know, they know. But it's all in her head. She's aware of this.

It's a few tram stops and a short walk to Merchants Quay. When she sees Maggie's bright yellow front door she weeps with relief. She's scared Steve will find her here, but that's just her stupid paranoia. Steve doesn't know where Maggie lives.

She has her bag, some money, her dignity. She has freedom.

And she has Maggie. With her friend at her side, she'll be invincible, just like she used to be before she started choking.

83

NOW

When Maggie gets home after her disastrous date, she's surprised to find Franny sitting on her doorstep, a large bag by her knees. She's got headphones on and her eyes are closed. Her hair is uncombed and she has streaks of mascara down her face. This is what they describe as "an Alice Cooper".

'Fran?' Maggie says, then realises she can't hear her because of the music she's listening to, so gently nudges her with her foot. Franny's eyes open and on seeing Maggie, her lip trembles and tears leak from her eyes, bringing more black streaks.

With her back to the bright yellow door, Franny looks like the subject of one of those arty photos, where everything is monochrome apart from the one pop of colour. Against the sunflower yellow, she has the pallor and contrast of white baby's breath flowers, or delicate lilies. She pulls her headphones off and says, 'I'm so sorry, Mags. I'd have phoned, but everything is fucked.'

Maggie's not sure if she's talking about phones and such, or something more.

Inside, Maggie makes them both a cup of tea. They're silent for a while; Maggie senses the conversation that will follow will be serious and she wants Franny to catch her breath and take her time. She's suspected for a while that something is wrong at home, but they've not really had the time to talk.

Franny breaks the silence first.

'I've left him, Mags.'

'I guessed as much.' Maggie blows on her tea. 'Did you have a row?'

'You could say that.' Fran pushes the sleeve of her jumper up: a series of bruises snake up her arm. She lifts the front of her jumper: fist-sized splodges of purple. And other marks, older, different stages of a rainbow of abuse.

'My God, Fran.' Maggie almost drops her teacup. 'Did Steve do all that?'

'Yes, but don't worry, this time I fought back. He won't be coming near me, or anyone else, again in a hurry.'

'What did you do? Is he okay?' It's strange to ask this, but there's something in Franny's eyes that scares Maggie. She's scared for her friend. Did she do something terrible she can't undo?

'He'll live,' Franny says, and it sounds like she's sorry about that fact. 'I kicked him really hard in his balls, and then hit him with the first thing to hand, which happened to be that fucking ugly football trophy he keeps on the mantelpiece. It may have been ugly but it was good quality, not one of those crappy light things.'

'Are you sure he's okay?'

'I saw him getting up as I closed the front door. He's going to be fine. But he's going to have a headache in the morning.'

Franny starts to laugh, which turns into crying, and Maggie gets up and hugs her for a long time while she tells her all the horrible things she'd been putting up with, and for how long.

'I can't believe I never noticed any of this, Franny. I can't believe I didn't see it. I wish you'd told me before.'

'Oh God, you've so much of your own stuff to deal with.' Franny blows her nose loudly into a tissue. 'I couldn't possibly put all this on you.'

'So, what... you lived with it in silence all this time? How've you been coping?' Guilt that her best friend didn't feel like she could have leant on her hits Maggie.

'I was self-medicating with gin, vodka, and online gambling. You know, jackpot games, roulette. On my phone mostly, but sometimes...' Franny looks down at her hands. '...sometimes at work on the computer. I was getting through a fair bit of money and it was a real problem, to be honest.'

'Oh, mate.'

'Hey, but good news about the world technology breakdown, eh? All joking aside, it forced me to stop relying on that crutch and to stand up and do something.'

'I'm so glad you did. You can stay here for as long as you like, and I'll help you as much as I can. My home is your home.'

Maggie realises that hope and home are just one letter apart, and she's happy she can offer both to the person who's been the most constant in her life outside her dad and granddad.

'Will you help me report him to the police?' Franny asks. 'But not now, not today. Let's get this weekend over and your granddad properly sent off.'

'Of course I'll help you, and thank you for understanding.'

They open a bottle of wine and, at least for this one evening, try to push everything away.

84

NOW

Maggie loves and hates the crocheted blanket. Those two emotions are fighting for her to hear their voices, but she keeps them locked inside her head. She doesn't want to let them out because neither one of them is going to be any use nor do her any good.

She loves the blanket because it lay on top of her granddad's bed for decades, and she hates it because it's now on hers, and she can still smell herbal tablets and Algipan, can still feel some warmth she knows is an illusion, but she wants to hold on to it all the same.

If you were making a human and wrote a list of all the great attributes someone could have, you'd start and end with love and in the middle would be all the other things her granddad was: patient, kind, funny, strong, fair. And they'd all be wrapped in a crocheted blanket that would absorb the smells that bring a person back to you when they're gone. The blanket was crocheted by Maggie's grandmother and each square of it was made during a period of her marriage. Maggie remembers it always being there. It's part of him. Was part of him.

She's taken it downstairs and is sitting with it over her knees as she drinks her coffee in her armchair by the window. She doesn't want to think about later today. If she doesn't think about it, and how it'll mark her loss, she'll be able to keep her memories, and him, alive for another day.

It's good to have another person with her. Franny makes herself indispensable by preparing coffee and a plate of toast, which they both pick at. Franny draws up a chair beside Maggie's at the window and they sit in companionable silence for a while. The sun has decided to shine over Manchester today, as if it's out to show its respect, and there's a warmth in its rays.

'Harold was a sound guy,' Franny says, and Maggie smiles. 'Always had a cheery word. Always a gentleman.'

'Yeah. He was the only one in my family who really supported me. The only one, I think, who believed me about everything. But...'

'But what?' Franny asks, puzzled.

'I found out the other day that he's been hiding something from me for eight years.'

Franny's eyes are wide. 'What?'

'A letter from my son. From Charlie.'

'Fucking hell. I don't believe it. That's huge.'

'You don't say. Yeah, it's a bit of a shocker.'

Maggie fetches the letter and gives it to Franny to read.

'This is unbelievable, Mags. So, you're going to contact him, right?'

'Yes, I'm going to contact him, if he's still in the same place. It looks like his parents' address, so they're probably still there. Hopefully.'

And it suddenly hits Maggie. She's found her son. Or almost, at least. She has an address. She has a chance. She has hope.

85

NOW

A small floral wreath, tied with a purple ribbon, is sitting on the grass a little way away from the rest of the family's flowers. Maggie bends to see the card that's tied to the top.

> *To Harold.*
> *You meant the world to me. Thank you for being far and away one of the best men in my life.*
> *Paul.*

Suddenly, she can't breathe. She's reminded of the lovely relationship Paul and her granddad had. After his uncle Bob died suddenly of a heart attack, Harold was the only constant and good male left in Paul's life.

She realises it's not just she who's losing all these people. Others are involved. Others are feeling pain and grief.

'Penny for them.' Paul appears, as if by magic, as if her thoughts of him are enough to invoke him. Maggie smiles.

'You could stand in for Mr Benn's shopkeeper,' she says.

'What?'

'Never mind, how are you?'

'I'm okay,'

Paul's face darkens and he looks away briefly. His gaze hovers over the flowers. The array is breathtaking. Pure white lilies, roses of all colours, pale cream chrysanthemums and orchids, formed into wreaths and stunning bouquets. Maggie hadn't expected so many, although she knows her granddad had many friends and was much loved.

And there are a few military men here, wearing their uniforms; younger than her granddad because all the men his age are already gone. His subordinates, she realises. They all have white hair and faces of malleable granite, like they're fighting with the hardness their career gave them.

Her gran is moving slowly among the wreaths, occasionally stooping very slowly and deliberately to read a card. She looks so serene, Maggie thinks, so beautiful, elegant and dignified.

'More to the point, how are you?' Paul asks and Maggie's attention is drawn back to him. 'After your revelation.'

But now isn't the time. The pall bearers are ready and it's time to say goodbye.

86

NOW

Funerals are strange things, Maggie thinks. She's standing in a church that's filled to the rafters with people who've come to witness her granddad's last journey, and they all look so splendid in their best clothes, and they all have such looks of love and sadness on their faces, but there'll be no record of this. Why don't people take photos at funerals like they do of everything else? Everywhere else in life, you can't move for people taking selfies, or photos of buildings, family groups, cute animals. They take photos of their food, of their new hairstyles, of their cups of coffee with cinnamon spice. They snap away at christenings, birthdays, weddings. But when it comes to the very last function for someone they love, no one ventures to get their phones out. Not that it would be much use right now.

She supposes in some ways it's a good thing. People rely so heavily on photos. They spend most of their existence looking at life through their phone screens, seeing it all in 320 x 480 pixels instead of the wide-angled, full-colour spectrum of real life. And in doing that, they miss everything. The brain's capacity for memory isn't tested fully when you know you have a photo to look at. But what happens when the technology you rely on fails? Which is what is happening now. That real-life picture you should have sent to your brain was never truly looked at, and so it's hard to keep it.

But Maggie will keep this forever, in the hard drive in her mind. There must be at least five hundred people here, and that's just inside this church. The one her grandparents married in, where they baptised Maggie's father and his brothers. So many people loved him.

The service includes a requiem mass and communion, so it's long but seems to pass rather quickly. Her gran is keen for Maggie to receive communion as she says it would have made her granddad happy and Maggie doesn't have the heart to refuse her, but when she gets to the head of the procession, she declines the host and asks for a blessing from the priest instead. She doesn't believe in any of it, is certainly not a Catholic anymore, but she reckons a sign of the cross from this man in a smock isn't going to kill her.

At the graveside after, during the Lord's Prayer, Maggie closes her eyes and tries to recall her granddad's face. It was always a cheery face which, considering the awful things he saw as a young man, was a miracle. But he was the kind of person who took the most from life, and the experiences he'd had. In that respect he was very much like Maggie's dad, who'd also taken what life gave him as a lesson to be learned, and who cheerfully made the most of everything. Two great men from the same block of wood.

Maggie watches the coffin as it's lowered into the ground. Another great man in her life has gone. That's two of them now. They're all leaving. She feels a sob rising up from the very pit of her stomach and just before it's released, someone grabs hold of her hand. She looks up. It's Paul. His hand is warm and it squeezes hers.

The third great man is still here.

87

THEN

Splitting up with Paul has been hard, mostly because Maggie can't explain it. She can't tell anyone it's the bear that broke them up; the presence of it under her bed and inside her chest, where often she can feel it breathing at a pace faster than she can take. It causes her to panic, hyperventilate, feel faint. She can't deal with anything when this happens and just wants to take to her bed.

Thank goodness for Franny, who is always there to drag her out of bed and make her stand up straight. Who listens to her cry about Paul, and allows her to be devastated by it, even though she was the one who finished it.

'He's the love of my life, Fran, but it's just too hard.'

'I know, I know,' Franny says, soothing Maggie, allowing her to rest her head on her shoulder on the sofa. 'I know why you're feeling like this, and I only wish I could help.'

Maggie knows her granddad told Franny about the pills and the wine on the night of her aborted wedding day and that this terrifies her.

'You are helping, just by being here.' And she means it. With Franny here, she'll be safe from herself.

But eventually, Franny has to leave, because Steve needs her. He doesn't like Franny to be away too long.

So, life goes on without him. For almost two years, she doesn't see him at all, and then one day she runs into him on Peter Street, and he's with a pretty young woman with a swollen belly and he has a wedding ring on his finger. They hug shyly, awkwardly, and Maggie feels her heart will explode with a thousand different emotions: sadness, regret, fear, deep love. He looks so good and well. And happy. It tears her to pieces this sudden and unbidden thought of him with someone else, making his life wonderful again. Making a future.

'What a sight for sore eyes,' Paul says when they release from the hug. He's unaware of his wife's curious and not-sure-that-I'm-happy expression. 'You're looking good, Mags.'

Hearing him say her name sends a jolt through her, which she pushes away.

'You too.'

"Are... are you a married man now?' She forces joviality into her voice. She puts her hands on her hips and addresses the woman in a bid to show her there's nothing to feel threatened about. 'You finally made this one settle down?'

She sees Paul close his eyes for a moment and feels his pain. She regrets her words immediately. Words carelessly chosen. She and he were settling down. And then she went and unsettled it all like throwing a tea tray filled with china cups all over the floor.

Paul laughs politely after the moment passes, and they pass a few more pleasantries until Maggie releases herself and says she has to get going because she's meeting a friend at the new coffee bar in Deansgate and she's already late.

In the café twenty minutes later, talking to her friend, she's shocked to see Paul looking in the window. Just standing there, looking in with a weird expression on his face, like he's an old man who's forgotten what he went into a room for. She excuses herself and goes outside.

'Paul?' she says and is uncertain he's heard her. But he looks up at her. His eyes are like liquid.

'I erm, I wanted to tell you my phone number is the same.'

'Paul...' Maggie's heart feels as though it will stop. 'Nothing's changed. I'm the same.'

She wishes she could tell him everything is different, and that she's sorry for hurting him and it would never happen again. But that would be a lie. The bear is still here. She wouldn't be able to help hurting him and she never wants to do that again.

'I know, but we can be friends, right?'

'I don't know if I deserve that,' she says, and it's true. She really doesn't.

But it looks like Paul does, and maybe that's enough.

88

NOW

'How are you holding up? That was a lovely service. God, Mags, you have so much going on. I can't believe what you told me the other day,' Paul says as he kisses Maggie on the cheek. They're at the buffet table and all round them, mourners in black are milling. There's a soft hum in the room.

'Charlie,' he says, shaking his head. 'Bloody Charlie. Who'da thunk it?'

'I know. I can hardly believe it myself. But I'm not building my hopes up, so stop being so excited.'

'Sorry, I can't help it.' Paul is filling his plate with mini sausage rolls and pork pies, crisps and chicken drumsticks.

Maggie snorts. 'So, your eating habits haven't changed.'

'Hey, my body is a temple to be worshipped.' Paul laughs, patting his stomach. It's a tiny bit paunchier, Maggie notices, but not much. She remembers worshipping at the temple. She remembers every inch of him. She shakes her head to rid it of the memories. This isn't the time or place.

'Hello, darling.' It's her mum. She's come over to the buffet table and picks up a plate. She offers her cheek to Maggie for a kiss, so she obliges. There's a faint smell of gin and peppermints on her breath, but she looks – for the first time in a long time – like she's made an effort and is dressed really nicely. She's even brushed her hair. Maggie is surprised and immensely grateful. She came through for the old man.

'Hi, Mum. How are you today?' There's tension in Maggie's voice she can't help. She needs to speak to her mum about the letter.

'Will you please excuse us?' she says to Paul, and she takes her mum's arm and steers her to a couple of chairs in a quiet corner of the room.

Without any preamble or warning, as soon as they're sitting, Maggie says, 'Gran found the letter from Charlie. I can't believe you kept it from me all this time.'

Maggie's mum is still holding her plate, but Maggie hadn't given her time to put anything on it. She raises it up slightly, turns it over, as if checking if any morsel of food might be clinging to the back of it.

'Are you listening?' Irritated, Maggie takes the plate from her mum.

'Yes, of course I'm listening.'

'And?'

'If you promise to calm down, I'll tell you.'

Maggie doesn't think she can calm down, but she spies Paul across the room and he's mouthing *listen*, so she does.

She listens.

89

NOW

'I'm so sorry, Maggie,' her mum says and she puts her hand on Maggie's.

Maggie jumps, shocked that she's calling her Maggie, and equally so at the touch of her hand. Her mother hasn't touched her for years.

'What do you mean, Mum? Sorry for what? Doing it or being caught out?' She wants to hear her explain. She wants to torture her and isn't proud of that. But the letter was something so important and she can't let this go.

It's as though they're stepping on the edge of something, like the Grand Canyon. She went there with Paul once, back when things were good, and Paul had made her keep her eyes closed and she'd let him lead her to the fence along the edge. He'd counted down – three, two, one – and told her to open her eyes, and she'd almost fallen to her knees with the sheer beauty of what she could see. A vast incredible hole in the earth that was a marvel of nature but had swallowed almost one thousand people over the years and taken their lives. Beauty tinged with terror. A place of life and death. And that's where she feels she is now, sitting with her mum at her granddad's funeral, feeling her soft hand on hers and hearing sorry.

Because in the saying of it, her mum is balancing on the edge.

And Maggie suddenly wants to keep back. No good can come of going there, to the outer reaches of that painful place. Like the Grand Canyon in its voracity, it'll eat her alive.

'Sorry about Charlie,' her mum says.

'Mum... don't.'

At the mention of his name, an unexpected jolt of pain erupts in Maggie's chest. It brings a memory that's more visceral than physical, like something has detached itself from her psyche. She remembers it *was* physical, if only briefly. Soft tiny mouth, palms and fingers flexing and pummelling gently, and a rhythmic *suck suck suck* noise. But now it feels like a false memory.

'No, I have to, Maggie, because if I don't, it'll mean I have to die with this inside me. This guilt. This sorrow that it happened at all, but mostly that it happened to you, my darling girl.

'I was so destroyed about losing your dad and everything that happened after that, I had no idea how to deal with it. What happened to you on the school trip was so against everything your dad stood for, against everything he ever protected us both from, that I didn't know what to do. So I shut it out. I pretended it wasn't true.

'And I'm so very sorry I said I didn't believe you. Because of course, I did. I do. But I was too scared to admit it even to myself.

'When the letter came, I panicked,' her mum is saying. 'All those years, and I thought it was behind us. Then there he was. In a letter. In my hand.'

'It was never behind me, Mum. How could you think I'd ever move on from it?'

'I don't know, darling. I can't explain it. I was scared. Of everything coming back. Of you getting hurt. Of me having the shame of it. Not *your* shame. Mine. The shame of failing you.'

'Oh, Mum!'

'I went to see your grandfather to get advice. He was the wisest person I knew, and I knew he'd have a solution. I remember he asked me what I believed would be the result of you getting the letter. He said it was a simple case of: would it help you or would it hurt you? Hearing it put so simply, there was no doubt in my mind that getting the letter would set you back years. Would bring back all the hurt. All the memories of what happened on the school trip. I didn't want you thinking of *him* again. I left the letter with Harold, so you'd never find it. I couldn't quite bring myself to destroy it.'

'But the hurt never went away, Mum.' Maggie is glad she didn't destroy it, but thinks her logic is skewed. 'I've never ever stopped thinking about the trip, about *him*, about everything. I'm seeing a therapist, for God's sake, *because* I can't stop thinking about it.'

'I know that. I do, really, deep down. I'm not stupid. I know stuff like that doesn't go away, although my solution for myself was to stifle and deny it. But... I saw you functioning. I saw you going about your life. After you and Paul broke up, you started, eventually, to put the pieces together. I couldn't risk you losing that.'

'It wasn't your choice to make though.' Maggie still can't believe her granddad thought that too, that they should make the choice for her. 'I had a right to know.'

'I don't know what else to say, darling. You know now. And everything that happens from this point will be totally up to you.'

90

THEN AND NOW

Maggie's father talks about mayflowers because he wants to get out in his garden but is unable to. He's too weak. He tells her that in spring the garden will be full of them and their sweet scent; that their colour will burn beauty into their eyes.

'You must keep them nice for me,' he says, and his eyes wander to the window. Maggie thinks he's going to say more but he doesn't. He just lets the thought drift away through the open window, through which the sound of birds and wind whisper through the bushes and hedges.

He leaves all the important stuff unsaid: the fact that spring is a long way away; the truth that he won't be here to see it. And because they're not said, the fact is still fiction and the truth is still a lie.

Maggie tells him when the mayflowers come up next spring, they'll both go and pick some nice ones and put them in a vase in the living room so the scent can fill the room. Fill the house.

'Mummy will love them,' she says, and watches a tear run down his cheek.

If she'd have known back then that that time with her father was going to be so brief and so precious, she'd have thrown herself at him and clung on. He left her life early and she was too young, too unknowing and too late to do anything about it.

But she and Charlie are still here.

Is it all up to her? It sounds easy when her mother says it like that, but it *feels* hard. There's a human, her son, who's walked around the world for twenty-three years not knowing he has a birth mum who loves him, who's never stopped loving him.

She'll put it right. It's not too late for them. And she can tell him all about his grandfather and great-grandfather so he can know them through her memories.

91

NOW

'How did the funeral go?' Taylor asks as Maggie brings her coffee over to the couch. She places it on the table and rummages in her bag, produces two Twixes. Taylor's eyes widen. She knows these are his favourite.'

'Want one?' she asks.

'Is the Pope Catholic?' he replies. Maggie hands one to him.

'It was okay,' she responds to his question. 'I couldn't believe how many people were there. He was a much-loved man.'

'And your family? Your nan and your mum. How did they bear up?'

'They were okay. My two surviving uncles were there, so Gran had lots of support. My mum showed up and was sober and washed, which is a bonus.'

'Did you speak to her about the letter and ask her why she kept it from you?'

'Yes, and I think we reached some kind of... stalemate about it. I'm not happy, but at least now I understand why. And I did a lot of thinking over the weekend about why my granddad kept it from me too. I realise he'd been the one to find me after my overdose and that must have scared him half to death. No wonder he worried about my state of mind.

'After the funeral, as soon as I got home, I wrote a letter in reply to Charlie's and posted it. Well, I guess I'll have to start practising calling him Simon now.' Maggie doesn't say her heart sinks a little whenever she thinks that her precious father's name didn't stay. She'll adjust.

For a while, there's silence in the room, broken only by occasional coffee slurps and contented murmurings at the Twixes. Taylor is scribbling away in his notepad. After about five minutes, he breaks the silence.

'There's something we haven't dealt with,' he says. He's flicking pages backwards and forwards, looking at something from way back in the notebook and then making marks on the page he's on.

'What's that?' asks Maggie, sucking on a finger of Twix.

Taylor looks right in her eyes.

'What happened to Mr Roberts,' he asks.

92

NOW

Maggie used to think of *him* all the time right after it happened and for so long. He occupied her nightmares, took up residence there, so he was with her every night, in her bed. With her every morning as she got ready for school and later, work. With her when she was with other people so sometimes she'd zone out and not hear them.

With her always.

She never reported him or told anyone at the school about what he did, and of course Franny was sworn to secrecy. She built up the courage to tell her mum, only to have her dismiss it and forbid her from mentioning it again. So, he lived inside her mind and could never come out.

After a while she thought of him less often, at least on a conscious level. He was relegated to being in the deeper recesses of her memory. He turned into the bear she still has to live with and step around.

At the end of the term after the Lake District trip, he left the school to become a gardener, get married and start a family. Maggie and Franny had done a secret happy dance in the playground when they heard, and Maggie was relieved she didn't have to look at him again. She heard his wife had twin girls and the thought made her physically sick.

'I stalked him for a little while a few years ago,' she says to Taylor. 'On Facebook. Which is crazy, I know. I can hardly fathom it myself, so I don't expect anyone else to understand it. Instead of reporting him to the police for what he did all those years ago, or going around to confront him, I just stalked him. I created a fake account and used a photo of a younger girl – I just picked it up off the internet. I'm ashamed of that. Using a photo of a real person to attract him.

'But he accepted my friend request and although we never spoke online or anything, I was able to keep an eye on him. Of course, he didn't do anything dodgy on Facebook. It looked like he had a family: two daughters. I wondered about them, you know.'

What Maggie means is tacit. Taylor nods, scribbles.

'Then, about a year ago, the bastard went and died. Fucking died, and I had to watch all the messages coming in on Facebook. How he'd be missed and what a great bloke he was. A loving father and a devoted husband. An inspirational teacher and a mentor. Franny had to practically hold me down to stop me going to the funeral. I wanted to go and stand at the back and shout how he was a paedophile and a rapist and they should ask his daughters if he fiddled with them. But of course, I didn't go.'

Taylor steepled his fingers and rested his chin on them. 'Sometimes, it's harder to let things go, but we have to, Maggie. You may regret not reporting him, but now it's done – or rather not done – and he's dead, it's too late. You can't go back and change the past, so you have to learn how to move on from it. You can do that by counting the blessings you have, if that doesn't sound too religious and spiritual. I don't mean it that way. I mean, look how far you've come. Look what great work you've done on yourself. By allowing all these terrible memories of the past to come, and by dealing with the way they make you feel in a measured way, you've conquered them. You're still here. You have family and friends, and you have love.'

He's right. She has so much. Her life-long best friend and partner, Franny; her gran; her mum, despite her faults; and Paul.

And soon, hopefully, Simon.

93

THEN

Confession is supposed to be therapeutic, and it's supposed to absolve you from your sins.

So, when Jim Roberts walks into the booth and sits on the seat – smooths his trousers out and picks off a hair – he's feeling fine. He's feeling confident.

'Bless me, father, for I have sinned,' he says, watching the head through the crimson curtain and hazy mesh nod sagely. 'It's six months since my last confession and these are my sins.'

He wonders who decides what's a sin and what's not a sin. Arguably, God, but he's not really sure he believes in God anymore. So... people on earth? The Pope? Bishops? Father Corrigan, the priest here at his school? But he's an imbecile.

He's going to leave them all behind anyway, have a change of career. His wife is expecting twins; they have a new home. They can make a new life. So it doesn't really matter what any of them here think. And before he goes, he can clear all the sin in his heart and take the huge weight off his chest.

Just in case God is real.

He tells the priest about his weakness because he knows he'll be forgiven. God made him, he tells the silent Father

Corrigan, and so gave him this weakness. God made the girl, with her beauty and her ways. Her allure. So, is it not God who's to blame?

He suppresses a smile. This box in which he's sitting is sacrosanct, holy, protected. He knows what is said in here can never be taken outside the wooden walls and won't follow him anywhere.

Father Corrigan doesn't speak for several moments. Jim Roberts looks at his watch, feels a twitch of hunger in his belly. He wonders what's for tea.

Then, Father Corrigan speaks.

'I want you to leave this confessional right now. I will not absolve you of this sin, and you will carry it with you.'

'What do you mean, you won't absolve me? Is it not your job to do so?'

'It most certainly is not my job to absolve and forgive that which is an abomination. I have my orders from God, and my orders are to protect the souls and the bodies of my flock. This is how I see my "job" as you call it.

'I strongly advise you to repent your sins and inform the authorities of what you have done. Then, and only then, will you be able to stand before me and God and be absolved. But I suspect you won't do that.'

If anyone should be punished here, Jim Roberts thinks, it's this incompetent priest. He knows his rights and is incensed.

He storms out of the confessional and through the startled group of other parishioners sitting or kneeling in the pews at the front of the church.

He needs to get away from this god-forsaken place.

94

NOW

There's an early autumn chill in the air. The hairs on Maggie's arm are standing up on top of gooseflesh. The sunshine is dark orange, becoming lower, casting longer shadows.

The pub garden is empty, so she has no trouble finding somewhere to sit. She chooses the table under a beech tree that's just starting to reveal the browning heart of its leaves, and sips her wine slowly. She doesn't want to have to buy another. She doesn't want to drink too much.

She touches the letter in her pocket. Without even seeing it she knows the colour of the paper, the width of the lines, the flourish and swirl of the words. She tries to imagine what the person who wrote them looks like; tries to see him sitting at a desk or table, with all the words inside him flowing from his mind, to his pen, to the paper. Tries to imagine what an eighteen-year-old boy looks like, what he thinks like, because she wants to think of him writing the letter. Wants to step inside his head.

But he's twenty-three now. A man. She's a mother to a grown adult.

When she wrote the letter to him all those years ago, she'd

hardly dared hope it would reach him, and never dreamed it actually would, let alone be answered. And although the reply was kept from her for so long, she has it now. Thank goodness his parents hadn't moved.

She keeps her eye on the door from the bar. It's busy here and it's opening all the time. Every man who comes out, she thinks it's him. Everyone is a possible because she doesn't know what he looks like. Will he be tall? Will he be handsome? What colour will his hair be? Occasionally, someone's eyes meet with hers and she wonders... but then they flick away, land on someone else with the light of recognition. None of them are for her, but every one makes her heart miss a beat from the possibility.

Back when she'd last held him to her, she'd kissed the sparse wisps of hair on top of his head. They were pale brown with a hint, a sparkling, of red. She always tries to push away the image of the man he came from, but she can't deny forever that some of him will be in the boy.

But she'll still love him, won't she? No matter what.

She's about to find out. The door is opening and a man is coming out. This time, when their eyes meet, the spark, the light, is for her.

Because she just knows. And so does he.

95

NOW

They hug. He feels her head against his, the weight of it on his shoulder, and the breath he's expelling is loud. But he can't help it. He's feeling something extraordinary and he knows it's crazy. This woman, who he's never met until now, is making him feel something powerful. He's connected to her as he's never been to anyone before.

His mum and dad have always given him love and affection, and he's not wanted for anything from them. Nor from the girlfriends he's had. Everyone tells him he's irritatingly lovable – it's a standing joke.

He's had plenty of hugs. But not like this one. Then he realises: he *has* met her before. She's his mother.

Her hand is at the back of his head and she strokes his hair. Then she releases and stands back, puts her hands on his face. Her eyes are sparkling and she looks like she's holding her breath, maybe for fear of what will come out. The hands on his cheeks are shaking. Her chest is heaving.

She's so beautiful, he thinks, with a rosy glow high up on her cheeks and a sparkle in her eyes – eyes he recognises from his own mirror, his own face.

'The first thing I want to tell you,' she suddenly says before he has a chance to say anything, 'is I love you so much. I always have. I didn't want to let you go but I had no choice.'

'I know that,' Simon whispers, but he doesn't think she's heard him. She has a speech; one she's probably been thinking of for twenty-three years. He's going to let her make it.

'But I remember the smell of you, the feel of you, and I've carried that memory with me since the day you were taken. You smell and feel the same. I know it's crazy, but you do. Maybe it's just my heart tricking my brain. I love you.'

They hug again and Simon realises this is the first day of something new. He has so many questions, and he knows she must too. So many missed years; two lives lived separately.

And now, against all odds and with all the challenges the world has been facing these last weeks, they're here. United again.

96

NOW

Maggie is helping Franny pack her stuff. Steve has grudgingly let them into the house and says they have thirty minutes then he's chucking them out. Maggie resists the urge to tell him to go fuck himself because she knows that will just antagonise him, and this is Franny's battle, not hers. She's learned to choose her battles wisely. And besides, she has enough of her own.

They get everything Franny wants to take and they lug it downstairs in the two suitcases they brought with them. As they reach the hallway, Franny grabs an envelope out of her bag and stands it on the hall table.

'My rings,' she explains to Maggie's inquisitive look. 'Don't want any reminders of the fucker.'

They've timed it well. As they're leaving a police car pulls up outside. Franny looks at Maggie.

'So, they're going to do it. A DVPN... to protect me.'

'Does that mean he'll have to move out?'

'Yeah, I think he has twenty-four hours. I mean, the house is mostly mine. My name was on the mortgage because he didn't want to get tied in.'

'Well, you can stay with me, of course, until he's out, and then we can get you back on your feet.'

They decide to go to the pub, so once all Franny's stuff is at Maggie's, they head to The Cage. This is the scene of many of their crimes over the years; their stomping ground and their safe haven. Every man in this pub would have beaten Steve half to death if they'd known what he'd been doing to Franny. Every man in here is a friend, an ally, a protector. But sometimes, it's not about being protected and saved by someone else. It's about protecting and saving yourself. And Franny is doing it.

As they sip their pints, there's something Maggie needs to know.

'Are you in any debt from the gambling?'

'A bit,' Franny admits. 'But not as much as it could've been, and I've almost paid it all back. I used my credit card mostly, which is stupid. But it was so easy to keep tapping on those buttons to refill and keep going. All those colours and noises; it made me feel drunk and happy. I couldn't stop.'

'Until you had to, right? With the phones crashing and that?'

'Yeah. God, Maggie, that was the miracle that saved me. The fact that I simply couldn't go on. And it got me thinking differently, and more clearly. It's what made me finally decide to leave. Oh, the beatings were part of the decision, but while I was still able to gamble, that was what was distracting me from those. And when that distraction was taken away, I was left with the stark truth and couldn't ignore or deny it anymore.

'I've started to think more about things, outside of myself. Stuff makes me cry now that never would before, because I never thought about them. But there are some incredibly sad things in the world and they aren't even all that remarkable, because they're a part of life.

'Like parents having to go to food banks and clothes banks

to get free stuff for their kids, and it's the kids, the poor, poor kids who I feel for, growing up in a scary world where their mum and dad can't afford to clothe them. I realise now how much I really wanted children, and it never happened. So maybe I can help those that need me. I'm going to London, to my parents. I can get myself together there and... London has many homeless and needy people.

'It's not all about me,' she jokes.

Maggie thinks this is a wonderful idea and tells her. She's so proud of her friend, literally changing the course of her life after veering for so long in one direction. It's really something to admire.

'What about when it all comes back though?' Maggie asks. 'The phones, computers. When they finally sort the issues out and everything returns. Will you be able to keep away from the apps?'

'I don't know. Part of me hopes it doesn't come back, but if it does... I have you to help me. Right?'

Maggie can't believe how privileged she feels to be able to help her friend, after all the years of being helped by her. She's sad Franny has something she needs help with. But the privilege remains.

'Always,' Maggie says. 'Always and forever.'

97

THEN

By this holy unction and through His great mercy may God pardon thee whatever sins thou hast committed through the power of sight.

Her skin is pale with a faint blush, like a ripe peach. Her hair is a honeyed cloud that will bring a storm to unsettle him. Beauty like hers is made to torment men like him. When she looks his way, in class, her eyes are full of trust and wonder, like she believes he'll bring something profound into her life: learning, experience, joy of discovery.

By this holy unction and through His great mercy may God pardon thee whatever sins thou hast committed through the power of hearing.

She says his name with something he feels is reverence, whenever he invites her to address him. And he invites her often: calling her name in class to answer a maths problem; asking her to come and write on the board and speak aloud the solution; asking her how her mother is keeping when he keeps her behind after class. Her voice is sweet and gently girlish and sometimes trembles with something he finds charming. Respect or fear? He thinks the two are the same.

And he hears her whimpers of fear when they're in the churchyard, and in the tent.

But he never hears "no".

By this holy unction and through His great mercy may God pardon thee whatever sins thou hast committed through the sense of smell.

Her young girl odour is intoxicating. Sweat and the onset of womanhood masked by White Musk and Sure roll-on. The scents make his nostrils flare, and they call to him. He can't ignore them.

By this holy unction and through His great mercy may God pardon thee whatever sins thou hast committed through the power of speech.

He tells her she's useless whenever she fumbles and shakes in his presence, because that makes him feel good, feel powerful. He tells his wife he has to stay after class to coach a young student who needs extra attention, but that he loves her and will be home in time for dinner. He tells the priest he's sorry.

By this holy unction and through His great mercy may God pardon thee whatever sins thou hast committed through the sense of touch.

Soft skin so smooth he can't resist it. It always feels best when she flinches.

By this holy unction and through His great mercy may God pardon thee whatever sins thou hast committed through the ability to walk.

His own legs take him into the tent, and out again, in the dead of night. His own legs take him in and out of the confessional box, in which he fakes contrition. His own legs carry him away from the school, the parish, his past life.

Sometimes his legs walk past a new school. Just looking.

...abandon us not in the hour of our death, but obtain for us perfect sorrow, sincere contrition, remission of our sins...

Jim Roberts dies receiving his faith's final sacrament, but he dies a liar and a coward. His family lay him in the ground not knowing this, and they mourn his loss, as all loving families do.

Maggie Milburn watches their grief from behind her fake Facebook wall, disguised as a seventeen-year-old with plaits. She feels something she can't explain. She thinks at first that she wants to swoop in and ruin his highly regarded reputation, make him pay, even if only after death. But then she realises she'll be shattering his family too.

When he dies the truth stays buried with him.

But Maggie will never forget.

98

NOW

Maggie has invited Paul, his boys, and Simon to her house for Sunday lunch because Franny has gone to visit her mum in London for the weekend to reset after all that's happened and the house is quiet. Even the bear is hiding away somewhere. She wants to fill it with love and light, for the first time in forever.

This is a massive thing today. The two most important men in her life have never been in the same room together. She's never been able to look at them both in the same glance, although in her mind, several times over the years, she's pictured them together. But that was a secret she never gave voice to. As soon as she met Simon, all she wanted was to introduce him to Paul. She could think of nothing more logical.

She knows Paul's favourite roast is beef – and his boys would eat a tortoise as long as it was smothered in gravy and had peas on the side. She has no idea what Simon's favourite is and never thought to ask him, but reckons beef is a safe bet. Then she wonders, what if he's a vegetarian, or worse still, a vegan? She goes into a mild panic, realising there's nothing in her kitchen that would pass as vegan, apart from the vegetables and maybe the champagne. Is champagne vegan? She vaguely remembers reading somewhere that Veuve stopped using finings and declared themselves suitable for vegans so that's okay.

'Jesus, Margaret, why on earth are you stressing about vegan stuff when you don't even know if he's a vegan,' she admonishes herself in a voice remarkably like her mother's. Great, now she's talking to herself and she's becoming her mum. She cracks open a can of lager to take the edge off her nerves.

With the beef cooking nicely and the potatoes and veg prepped, she allows herself to breathe. And when everyone arrives, she finds she has nothing to worry about, because Simon is as much of a carnivore as everyone else and tucks into the beef like he's not eaten anything for years, although Maggie can see he's been well looked after and is healthy and happy.

When she introduces him to Paul, the two men hug, and something inside Maggie twangs, like someone is pulling an elastic band inside her chest. It's not an unpleasant feeling. It's like that elastic band is being fastened, at last, to something on the other end, and the tension signifies being anchored, connected. Like the umbilical cord has been somehow reattached.

'I thought I'd never find you,' Simon tells her when they're washing the dishes together after the meal. 'When mum gave me your letter when I was eighteen, it took a few days for it to sink in, but I wanted to write back to you straight away. When I didn't get a reply, I thought that was that. Maybe you'd moved away, or just didn't want to revisit the past. I thought I'd never have another chance. But then, five years later, I watched a TV programme about tracing people through DNA, and after that, ads started popping up on Facebook, like they do when you've been talking or thinking of something. Like magic, right?'

'It seems like magic to me,' Maggie says, and she touches his arm as he dries a plate.

'And then I get a response. The results of the test, and I'm thinking this is it. I might have answers in here. Relatives who'll lead me to you.' He smiles at Maggie. 'But then, everything gets wiped away before I have chance to find out.

'That we are here today, because of your gran finding that letter, is nothing short of a miracle.'

Maggie cannot disagree with that, although she doesn't believe in miracles, or things happening for a reason. Things just happen, and there are happy – ecstatic – accidents. And this is one of them. Although she's mad at her granddad for keeping the letter from her, she also silently thanks him for not throwing it away and for keeping it in the box under his bed.

She doesn't want this day to end, but soon, Simon has to leave.

'I promised I'd have tea with Mum,' he says, then his eyes dart away, as if he's sorry to have used the word. 'Thanks so much for today, though. I had a really wonderful time. Paul is ace.'

'Yes, he is. That's perfectly fine,' Maggie says, despite wanting to say it's not really fine. It will be, one day, but right now, it's hard thinking of another woman being his mum.

'May I call you Mom? I call Mum Mum, so...' Simon says, his face open, expectant.

Maggie can't believe it. Her heart wants to burst open.

'It's what they use in Birmingham, which is where my mum's parents are from,' Simon explains.

'Of course you can. Of course. Come here.' She pulls him toward her and hugs him; feels his hair against her cheek. 'I can't tell you how long I've waited for you to say this to me. My boy. My darling son.'

99

NOW

'It's Stephanie Wilson's funeral next week,' Maggie says. She throws a glance over to Aaron, but he hasn't heard. He's building a tower with her Jenga. George is beside him, on the sofa, flipping through a picture book about Tudor kings and queens.

Aaron had confessed to his dad a few days ago that for a while he was being mercilessly bullied via WhatsApp.

'I can't believe I didn't see it,' Paul had said to Maggie when he told her. She'd assured him that often these things go unnoticed, and thank heavens for the recent respite. It could've been a lot worse.

But now, Aaron is here and it's great to see him looking so happy, so she doesn't want him to hear this. She beckons Paul away into the kitchen.

'It's so tragic, what happened to her,' she says as she fills the kettle. 'And it's not the first time this kind of thing has happened.'

'Is this the soap actress who was ripped apart by social media wolves?' Paul asks. Maggie nods. 'God, yeah, what is it with people?'

Maggie is feeling particularly torn about Stephanie Wilson. She was an actress who'd made the mistake of revealing she'd had an abortion when she was seventeen, because she wanted to take up an amazing acting opportunity. She hadn't been married or in a relationship, and her parents couldn't afford another mouth to feed. So, she'd agonised and made the decision she'd felt was right for her at the time. Though she was – supposedly – a national treasure and a "people's favourite" actress, she'd been hounded on social media and lambasted for her choice, which forced her to delete her accounts. Eventually, it led to this tragic end to such a young life.

'Aren't we supposed to be evolving as a planet, as a race, as decent human beings?' Paul says. 'Doesn't that mean learning to care about other people? About how they feel? If you woke up every day with dread, wondering what someone was going to say about you today – what lies they were going to invent about you, what assumptions they were going to make based on absolutely zero knowledge of you – would you enjoy that?'

'Absolutely not.' Maggie can't think of anything more awful.

'Right,' Paul says. His brow is furrowed. 'I don't believe anyone who says they don't care what people think of them. That's just a self-defence thing, a two fingers up to life to disguise the pain they really feel. If you don't feel it when someone is being mean to you, when they're being hateful, then I'm sorry, I think you're dead inside. I went through enough of that, and watched my mother go through that. Watching someone beat them down. Not in the same way people do today, but still...

'So, if you wouldn't like to wake up every morning feeling that way, you should care that other people don't. Kindness is seen as a weakness rather than a strength these days. Can you believe that? People are called "woke" or "snowflakes" for actually giving a shit about other people and how they feel.'

Maggie's always been amazed at the man Paul turned into, considering his supposed role model for a man. He totally connects with kindness; it runs through him, like a stick of rock from Blackpool. The image makes Maggie smile. This man is her stick of rock. Definitely her rock; her anchor to life.

Paul is still going: '"Political correctness gone mad" said no kind person ever! What's wrong with it? What's wrong with being aware of other people's feelings? How many people have to take their own lives after being ripped to shreds by the unwashed masses hiding behind their keyboards, screens and phone? How many? I'm glad we had these outages. I'm glad it stopped. I hope it never comes back.'

Maggie doesn't know if it'll ever come back. Either way, it's far too late for Stephanie Wilson. Thank goodness it wasn't for Aaron.

100

NOW

'It's not been so bad, this mysterious tech failure,' Maggie says. She reaches for the last biscuit at the same time as Paul, and for a second they have a mini tug of war. They both laugh. Talking about the soap actress who was taken too soon dampened the mood earlier, but now they're in the living room, on the sofa, and Paul's sons are playing quietly together. So, they feel happier.

'What? You're telling me not having your phone for several weeks hasn't been bad? You? The woman who can't go for a pee in the middle of the night without checking her socials?'

Maggie takes a swipe at him, but she can't help smiling. Mostly because his reference to her nocturnal scrolling is a nod to the intimacy they once shared, and it makes her feel warm inside.

She remembers feeling safe with him, always. Safety was never the issue. Love was never the issue. She loved him dearly. She still does. Loving him, and being loved by him, is something she'll never take for granted. He's helped her through so much: her grief about her dad, Charlie, her mother's depression and their strained relationship. And now Gramps. Paul's such a beautiful soul. And he'd believed her. That was everything.

If only things were different. If only *she* were different. Half of her wants more than anything to be with him again in every way a person can be with someone else. But the other half knows she has a lot more healing to do before she can be with anyone.

Maybe the next thing she should do, since she's been so honest in her therapist's office, is to be honest with Simon. It's terrifying, wondering whether to be up front about the exact way he was conceived, and she's so unsure. So unsure...

'Yeah, well, I've changed,' she says, pushing aside the deep sadness that's threatening to wrap her in its grip. 'I can see the benefits.'

'What do you think caused it, Mags?'

Maggie thinks for a moment. There have been many theories, mostly from the tin-foil hat brigade. She doesn't want to subscribe to any conspiracy theories, like Russia trying to kill the world, which actually, could well be true, or aliens trying to send radio waves that would zap a person as they used their phones. But in her heart she wants to believe it was something good, something beautiful, that happened. A nice conspiracy theory.

'I think it might have been the universe trying to heal itself – don't laugh.'

'Why would I laugh?'

'Because it's hokum, right? The universe? I know how crazy it sounds, and I don't even know if I really believe it, but I want to. I really do. I had this dream the other night and in it, the universe was like an orchestra playing beautiful music.'

'Ah,' Paul said, around a mouthful of Hobnob. 'The music of the spheres. I've heard of that.'

'Yes, beautiful music, coming in waves. But you can't

actually hear it with your ears. Or at least, in my dream I couldn't. It's your soul that hears it. It heals you, I think. That's what people say. Philosophers and the like. People much cleverer and more insightful than me.'

For some reason she can't understand, tears well up in her eyes. Whenever she thinks of something beautiful, it brings with it the pain of loss; of not being able to share the beauty with her dad, or with Charlie – Simon – for all these years.

'You know Mr Khan, my client with all the weddings?' Paul nods. 'Well, he's a Muslim and he's such a lovely, caring and kind man who makes me think so much of my father. He reminds me of him in so many ways.

'And I realised... they both believe or believed in God. A different God, and we may not believe like they do, but their belief gave them the same convictions and goodness. They both had and have faith in the beauty they believe their God created. That's such a powerful thought, don't you think? Believing in beauty?'

'I suppose it is,' Paul says. He has a strange look in his eyes, and it stops Maggie in her tracks a little.

'What?' Her cheeks flush pink. Paul reaches out and strokes her face.

'Sorry.' He pulls his hand back. 'I just... can't believe this is real. That you're here with me. It's twelve years later and you're here. Still with me. When I look at you, I believe in beauty, God or not.'

Something in Maggie's chest flutters, and her first instinct is to make light of what he's said. Make a joke. But she decides instead to ignore it and keep talking.

'I think the world lost its beauty, probably a long time ago. It became ugly. Because of people. Because of the arrogance we have over the things we've achieved, and the way in which we abuse them.

'Technology. It does so much good. So much. It finds diseases and saves lives, and reunites families, and stops people feeling so lonely. But it also does really bad things. It allows people to be hateful and cruel and cold without having to face the consequences. It makes people become addicted to things that tear them and their families apart – pornography, gambling.

'Along with all the good things, the nice things like the texts and emails to loved ones, and the photos of precious memories, there's also hate messages and photos posted on social media with the intent to shame and ruin lives. All those ugly things.

'Maybe some beautiful musical waves were sent to heal and calm our planet's troubled situation. Maybe our planet was reset.'

Paul sighs and Maggie thinks he wants to say something. Something his mouth won't let him say so it's only letting the air out. She knows him, though. She knows he will say what's on his mind.

'I want to believe what you're saying is true,' he says at last, 'because it's beautiful and poetic and noble. But I can't help wondering, what about you, Mags? Why can't it reset you? Why can't it reset us?'

101

NOW

On the morning after having Simon, Paul and his sons for lunch, Maggie wakes up to something she's not felt for a long time: silence and solitude.

Usually, when she wakes, she's acutely aware of the bear in the room, in her heart, in her mind. It cuts through every thought, every action she performs, from cleaning her teeth to eating her food; to speaking to people face to face; to going back to bed.

The severity and clarity of its presence usually varies throughout the day, but it's always palpable. The absence of it brings a surprising sense of panic, like the panic of realising you left the oven on and you're now a hundred miles from home.

After talking to Paul last night, Maggie came to realise a few things, not the least of which was that she needs to make the decision about whether to tell Simon about what happened to her. She realises this is the source of the panic. So, this morning she's weighing up the pros and cons of telling Simon the truth; has in fact made lists.

PROS OF TELLING SIMON

- We will be off on the right foot from the start
- Will be free of the fear of him finding out sometime
  – rip off the plaster!
- Will have support from Paul and Franny
- It will explain why he was given up for adoption
- It will bring us closer together

CONS OF TELLING SIMON

- He will know his biological father is a monster
- He might think it was my fault
- It will drive us apart

She realises the bottom line – literally on her lists, and figuratively – is that telling Simon will be make or break for them. But then, what is a relationship if not built on trust? Is it right to start something so important on a lie?

She doesn't have the answer to that question, but she does know she can't do it alone. She picks up her landline and calls Paul on his. She needs him here.

Right after calling him, she calls Simon. It's time.

102

NOW

Almost two weeks into an unprecedented worldwide technology outage, spokespersons from all major computer hardware and software companies have today assured normal services will be resumed early next week and all lost data restored.

The cause of the failures has not been officially confirmed, and many are saying we may never know the cause, but "workarounds" have been created and tested, and our lives will be put back on track next week, according to sources on the inside.

Some people are saying they prefer the new peace and quiet of a technology- and media-free world, but others are saying they can't wait to get back to talking to their loved ones far away and catching up with their "socials".

The companies who provide storage and media platforms have pledged a two-month grace period from billing, with payments recommencing in November.

103

NOW

'What's up, Mom,' Simon says as he walks through the door of Maggie's flat. Maggie feels a frisson of delight at the word she'll never stop loving the sound of. 'You only saw me yesterday. Everything okay?'

'Oh, I just wanted to talk to you about something.' Maggie tries to make it sound light, but it comes across as fake; she can hear it herself.

Simon shrugs off his coat, and his brow is furrowed, deepening when he sees Paul is in the flat too. He accepts Maggie's offer of a drink and looks surprised when she pours three large whiskies.

'Do I need this?' Simon asks when she hands it to him. There's a laugh in his voice, but Maggie can also hear worry.

Maggie's lost count of all the times she worried when her Charlie – as he was then – was taken. In the weeks and months that followed, her mind obsessed about where he was, who had him, how he was being treated. She lived in permanent darkness and greyness; shut herself away in her room and ventured out only sometimes to eat.

One day, about six months after he'd gone, her mother

forced her to open her bedroom curtains, and she was blinded by the sunshine streaming in. The warmth of it on her face brought something that felt like an old memory – of her and her dad, in Blackpool, sitting in a café eating donuts with hot summer sun streaming through the window. Back then, she worried about him; his illness. When he died, she worried about her mum. When she got pregnant, she worried about the unborn baby, and when he was born, she knew she'd never stop worrying.

Because that's the thing about loving someone. They become a thing to worry about forever.

'Are you my dad?' Simon is looking at Paul as if a penny is dropping, something falling into place. He also looks as if this news would be very welcome. There's a tiny cautious smile of expectancy on his face.

'I'm afraid not, mate,' Paul says, and Simon's face drops. 'I didn't know Maggie back then. She was very young. I wish I *had* known her.'

A look passes from Paul to Maggie and its warmth is palpable. She looks back at him with a smile, feeling a lump the size of an orange in her throat. She wants to weep with the knowledge that if she'd known him back then, none of the bad stuff would have happened.

But Simon wouldn't exist.

They sit down and drink their whisky in silence for a few minutes. Maggie can see so many questions in Simon's eyes. His eyes are the same eyes as her dad's. She has so much to tell him about; so many years lost in which she experienced things without him. He never would have known his granddad even if he hadn't been adopted and had stayed with her, but she can tell him all about the great man he was. And she can tell him all about Paul.

'Your biological father wasn't a good man,' she says, thinking that just coming out with it is the best policy. She sees Simon's eyes narrow, like he has a million questions. But he doesn't speak. Just looks at her with an unwavering gaze. She continues.

'Back when I was at school, something happened to me. I was... raped by a teacher. It resulted in me getting pregnant, and when you were born, it was... decided that you'd be given up for adoption.'

She thinks this is enough. Simon has already read her letter, already knows she never wanted to let him go. But she feels she must explain the most important thing.

'But I want to tell you again, as I did the day we met, that you were always loved. From the moment I saw you. I never want you to doubt that. You were, and are, everything to me. I never thought of you as a part of *him* at all. There's nothing of him in you. Nothing. He's never had any right to be a part of you.'

'Oh, Mom, I'm so sorry.' Simon rushes to her and hugs her. 'I can't believe such monsters exist. Were you okay? Are you now?'

Maggie can feel his tears on her cheeks.

'I'm doing great, my darling. Now.' Maggie looks at Paul. 'A lot has been happening lately, and I've been getting help. But the best tonic and medicine in the world has been you.'

And she knows she's never spoken a truer word. Her life is almost complete.

104

NOW

Paul watches Maggie close the door to Simon, and the sight of her makes his heart swell to about twice its normal size. She looks so beautiful, with slightly flushed cheeks and eyes all sparkling and liquid from her tears. Ever since she told him about Roberts, and Charlie being taken, he's admired her even more than he did when he first met her. Every bone in her body and every inch of her skin is noble and dignified. Even in tumultuous moments in their relationship, when they argued, he'd always find a second to look at her and marvel at the way she's put together.

Today, she's done a difficult thing and has still come out of it looking fucking marvellous. A warrior.

'Mags,' he says, as she turns from the door to come back into the apartment. She stops short on seeing him looking at her. He wonders what his face looks like. If it's anything like his heart feels it'll be crumpled and twisted and anguished.

'Yes? Are you okay?'

'I don't think I am.'

How can he explain to her that without her, he's half the man he used to be? Even with two beautiful sons. Some days it's all he can do to stop himself telling her he wishes with every breath that Aaron and George were sons from her. That they'd had kids. That their life together hadn't ended abruptly because of something neither of them could control.

Maggie comes towards him and takes his hand, leads him to the sofa. It's like she knows how he's feeling, that he's delicate, that he needs care. They both sit.

'Thank you for being here today, and every day,' she says, and she keeps hold of his hand in both of hers. She's looking him right in the eye. 'I don't know what I did to deserve you.'

'The privilege is all mine,' he says. And it is. 'When I first met you, I could sense you were harbouring something, and at first I thought it was something you needed protecting from. Franny certainly thought so.'

'Ha!' Maggie laughs. 'And she certainly did a good job. Maybe I did need protection.'

'Ah, maybe... but I don't think so. What I think you needed was space, and time.'

'You sound like Captain Kirk.'

They laugh, and Maggie holds his hand tighter. 'It's bloody fab though, that I found him, isn't it?'

'It's the best thing ever, Mags, because it's lit you up.'

'I feel lighter than I have in years,' Maggie says. 'Going to see the therapist helped more than I'll admit to Franny... but seriously, it helped clear up so much. Just saying a lot of the stuff out loud helped me make sense of it and see that nothing about it was going to change. Things that happen in the past can never be undone, so you have to make the decision to move on from them, otherwise they'll destroy you.'

'Have you moved on from us?'

The question surprises even Paul because he didn't know he was going to ask it. He's wanted to, for a long time, but never dared. Now he has. But she doesn't answer.

'You know,' he says, and he looks Maggie straight in the eye, 'all day, every day, I dream about what could have been if your dad hadn't died so young, if Roberts had never been born, if you and I had made it.'

Maggie opens her mouth to speak, but he rushes on before she can say anything: 'But I know that's stupid. Like you said, all those things happened and can never be taken back. And Simon was born. Look at the man he is now. He's fucking incredible. And you're right, Roberts has nothing to do with him and never will. And my boys – oh, they're just too perfect for words and I'd die for them.

'But... but... I dream about if all the things got thrown into a pot and mixed up, and you and I had got married, and had Simon, and then Aaron, and then George.'

'Oh, Paul. I...'

'No, don't say anything.' Paul closes his eyes. 'Let me sit with this dream for a little while longer.'

105

NOW

Maggie can feel the heat transferring from Paul's shoulder to hers as they sit side by side on the sofa. She can hear a distant thud and she's not sure if it's her heart in her chest, or Paul's heart in his. Maybe a combination of both.

'When you came to that café,' Maggie says, breaking the silence, 'that day we met in Peter Street, I had to stop myself from jumping into your arms. I was so happy, and I kind of knew you'd do it. That you'd follow me.'

'Why didn't you jump into my arms?'

'You were married. You had a baby on the way.'

'That's not all that's kept you from me, Mags. I've been divorced for a few years now.'

Bumping into Paul that day and seeing the way he was moving on was a huge blow that took Maggie off her feet, then and for a long time after. She'd not exactly expected him to curl up into a ball in the corner and never see anyone else again, but she'd not been prepared for seeing him with another woman.

'Well, what did you expect? You moved on. You got married.' Inexplicably, anger and irritation has entered Maggie's voice. She pulls away from the back of the sofa, from Paul and sits up; puts her face in her hands.

'Were you mad at me, Mags? *Are* you still?'

'I've no right to be, but yes, I was and I don't know if I still am. I left you. I let you down. But I didn't expect you to accept it quite as easily as you did.'

She can't explain it. It's crazy. She didn't want him to come charging after her like a bull, but his silent acceptance was tough to take. She glances back at him on the sofa and sees a look of such incredulity on his face, it almost makes her laugh. Instead, she smiles.

'I know, I know, I'm a crazy woman, right?' She's relieved when she sees the crack of a smile at the corner of his mouth. 'I can't give you any explanation other than the reason I ran from our wedding was because I was too fucked up, and then, when you accepted it, I kind of wished you'd stayed to help me fight everything.'

'When we met up again, and when we started seeing each other and hanging out, I felt like everything might be well again, but of course it wasn't. Everything was still there. Nothing had changed. Which is why, even when you split with Louise, I still couldn't allow us to get together.'

'You have tickets on yourself, don't you? I never asked you.'

Maggie knows he's joking here, but his voice is flat like he can't force the obvious humour into his mouth.

'Was it my fault? You and Louise,' Maggie asks, and she can't look him in the eye.

'I wish I could tell you no, so you'd not feel bad, but... yeah.' Maggie thrusts her face in her hands again. 'But not because we met up again on Peter Street.'

Maggie's not sure she's heard that right, and doesn't understand.

'If not that, why? Why did you break up? It must've been because we were seeing each other, even just as friends.'

'No.' She does look at him now and his eyes are glistening and full. 'No, Mags. It's not because we met up in Peter Street. It's because you exist. It's because I met you over twelve years ago in The Cage, when you were dancing like a lunatic and drunk as a skunk on red wine, and you were so fucking amazing and precious that you had a bodyguard prepared to kill a man with her bare hands for you. It's because you breathe. It's because you are. I don't know any other way to say it.

'Louise and I broke up because I've never loved anyone in my life as much as I love you, and I never will. And being with her was a bookmark, saving a place in my life until you picked me up again.'

Maggie can't breathe. She's watching tears roll down Paul's cheeks. She wants to hug the life from him. But she's frozen. 'Is that what you thought? That I put you down, Paul, to pick up again?'

Paul shakes his head. She takes his hand and leans back again.

'My dad always told me I could do anything, be anything, go anywhere. So, I always believed I could sort out my problems by myself. But I got a little lost along the way, thinking I had to shut out everyone else.'

'No one is an island, as John Donne said.' Paul smiles. 'Do you think you can recognise that now and let me help you? Let me help you get better? Let me help you reset?'

When she thinks of all she's been through, Maggie is overwhelmed, but so much good has happened in the last few weeks that, at last, she can see a chink of light in the heavy curtain.

And here, on the sofa with her, is the man who can help

throw those curtains open so all the brightness comes in. Just like her mother did that day, months after Simon had gone and she'd just been lying in bed every day.

Those days were some of the most miserable of her life.

106

NOW

The truth of that time, after Simon was born, was she was physically and emotionally drained. Her body had not been able to move after the pain it had endured. She'd not been ready for that. Not ready for childbirth: the cramping, the pushing, the ripping, the agony of realising this love wasn't meant to be. Wasn't *allowed* to be.

So she stayed in bed, day after day, watching dust motes in the spear of light her closed curtains let in. They'd billow and dance in the air like tiny Tinkerbells from *Peter Pan* and she'd watch for endless hours, wondering if her baby would ever see Peter Pan and Tinkerbell. Wondering if he'd be in a nice place and not the same hell she was.

When Maggie thinks of love, she always thinks of pain, because to her the two are always joined. You love your father, he dies. You love your baby, he's taken. You love a man... he'll never quieten the demons and you'll push him away.

She knows this is twisted. She wants to change it. She *is* changing it.

She remembers feeling safe, from time to time, when the bear wasn't there. She remembers waking up with the feeling of another human being wrapped around her; the warmth of skin on skin like liquid silk.

Now, she wonders what it would be like to feel all that again, and to deny the bear the power to take it away.

Paul's not the hero on a white horse her mother always said would come, but he's gentle and patient, and he makes her heart jump every time he's near her. She thinks he might be able to jump-start her heart back to life.

But, for now, she needs to be quiet with him in this strangely quiet world.

'You do know, don't you, Paul, that there's a hole in my heart where my father should be? You know I'll always have that?'

'I do know,' he says, and his hand goes to her back, gently stroking. 'And I know about all the other things. Roberts, Simon, your mum. Everything. But I'll help you.'

She wonders if he can help her. She knows he loves her, and it's a love that fills her up completely. She's loving the feel of his hand on her back, remembers the early days of their relationship, when their touches were electric and caused seismic shifts in their world.

'I'll let you help me,' she says. 'I do love you.'

It might not work out, but she knows she wants to try. When she's with Paul, her life makes the most sense. She hears him expel his breath; his relief is a living thing in the room with them, hesitant but creeping forward like an animal that doesn't know if it'll be fed or kicked.

'It's all I've ever wanted,' he says gently, cautiously. 'Not to rescue you, but to help you rescue yourself.'

She recalls his earnestness, from the start, that she be her own rescuer. He always stood back to let her reach her own realisations, but was always there at arm's reach.

'Well, okay then,' she whispers. 'Let's give it a go.' The urge to throw herself on him with tears of relief and gratitude is strong, but she resists it. Even though her heart is bursting from her chest, she takes a deep breath and quiets it, quiets herself. She simply grabs his hand and leans back with him on the sofa.

She rests her head on his shoulder, and they both close their eyes and sit for a while.

ACKNOWLEDGEMENTS

Thank you to: Betsy, Tara, Abbie, and all at Bloodhound Books for making my first experience with you such a dream and for producing a beautiful book; to Tracy Fells for your invaluable, unending support, friendship, and encouragement; to Joanna Campbell for your time and generosity; to my writing friends far and wide, especially Time to Write Club who make me so productive; and to my family, especially husband Keith Voisey, who mostly keeps out of my way when I need quiet.

ABOUT THE AUTHOR

Debbi Voisey is the author of two novellas-in-flash; Only About Love (Fairlight Books) and The 10:25 (Flash: The International Short-Short Story Press), both published in 2021 and available from the publishers and from Amazon. She writes novels, short stories and flash fictions, and is widely published in print and online. When she is not writing, running workshops, editing people's work and offering feedback, she likes to travel with her husband to Skiathos, her happy place. She also spends a lot of time in Manchester, which is where she gets a lot of inspiration. She has a website at www.debbivoisey.co.uk

A NOTE FROM THE PUBLISHER

Thank you for reading this book. If you enjoyed it please do consider leaving a review on Amazon to help others find it too.

We hate typos. All of our books have been rigorously edited and proofread, but sometimes mistakes do slip through. If you have spotted a typo, please do let us know and we can get it amended within hours.

info@bloodhoundbooks.com

Printed in Great Britain
by Amazon

61315496R00161